THE WHITE HORSE

CYNTHIA D. GRANT

mammoth

CHAPTER ONE

We're flying down the road in this big old car, my mother at the wheel, a Marlboro in her mouth, the windows open, hair blowing all around, her pink arm spreading out the window.

"Wanna see this thing do a hundred?" she says.

She cranks up the radio. It's howling.

I've just learned to count to one hundred in school. We're headed there now. The little arrow zooms up. Forty, fifty, sixty. The country road becomes a runway. We hurtle through a world of streaming color. The Buick shudders as if it will fly apart, pieces shooting into space; tires, doors, my heart. Seventy, eighty, ninety, one hundred. One hundred miles per hour in a ton of creaking metal, the engine screaming, one hundred and ten—

"Shit." My mother's fooling with the tape deck, hunting all over for her favorite cassette, looking through stuff on the floor, the dashboard. I'm steering with my eyes. She slams in the tape. A torrent of distortion blasts out of the speakers; her theme song, the music she hears in her head when things get broken and out of control, cops pounding on the door in the middle of the night.

"Where's the stewardess?" she jokes. "I need a drink."

My mouth opens and closes. No sound comes out. Like that goldfish we had. No plants, no friends. No food, sometimes, when my mother forgot. Or sometimes it ate ten times a day because we all wanted to feed it; we'd never had a pet. I'd watch that fish's mouth open and close and wonder what it was trying to tell me.

Help.

"This baby handles great," my mother shouts, feeling in her purse for a cigarette. Usually the backseat's full of kids, poking and pinching and slugging each other, until my mother hits like a meteorite; out of the blue, and hard.

I've never been alone with my mother before. And I'm thinking: We're going to die.

The city limits sign suddenly looms ahead. She punches the brakes and the cigarette lighter. We sail into town at thirty miles per hour, our SUPPORT YOUR LOCAL POLICE DEPARTMENT bumper sticker flapping, past the disappointed cop who's waiting for speeders. She waves at him; he doesn't wave back.

We cruise the main drag to the elementary school. I'm late, again, but they won't ask for a note. If they do my mother will pound on the counter and shout QUIT PICKING ON MY KID. Nobody messes with these kids but her.

She steers that boat into the parking lot. Such a tiny little lot, full of teeny toy cars. She slams on the brakes;

2

the engine's running, gunning itself, crap pouring out the muffler.

A woman walks by and shoots us a look, but scurries away when she sees my mother's face. She's never lost a fight, and I've seen plenty, like the one last night with the badass biker. He said she'd burned him; he wanted his money back. His friends had to carry him out.

"Bye, Mama."

She lets me kiss her cheek. I hop out and wave, but she's already gone, peeling rubber, like the cops are coming. They probably are. She hits the boulevard, tires screeching, as if she's just remembered something important, something crucial, like: I'M OUT OF DOPE.

I used to wonder: How can she do so much crank and still be fat? Most of the speedfreaks I knew were scrawny; skin stretched tight over skeleton bones. My mother gobbled down buckets of food: fried chicken, fish and chips, chili dogs, cheeseburgers, washed down with Coke, at least a case a day; some plain, some fortified with "Vitamin A," rum or vodka or whatever was around. She liked beer too and seldom got drunk; the drugs kind of balanced things out. She hated pot. Pot made her mellow. She didn't want to relax; she had to stay on guard because people could turn on you any second. Even the people who said they loved you. She didn't trust anyone enough to pass out.

The teacher stopped reading. From across the desk she could feel the girl's eyes on her face, like hands.

She chose her words carefully. "This is remarkable, Raina. It's even more moving than your poems."

"It's bullshit. Just a bunch of words."

The teacher's head snapped back as if she'd been slapped. But she kept coming, she was stubborn.

"Raina, why do you act like this? Why can't we talk?"

"About what?"

"I didn't know you'd lived in the country."

"We been everywhere. It didn't work out." She shoved a Marlboro into her mouth.

"You can't smoke in here."

Got it lit. Exhaled.

"You're a smart girl, Raina, with genuine talent. You can do something with your writing. Your life."

"This is my life. Real pretty, isn't it." She grabbed the pages, crumpled them up, threw them into the trash and walked out.

Chapter two

I am not cut out for this. I'm a lousy teacher. The kind who uses the word "lousy."

I am so discouraged. I want to quit. I am starting all my sentences with "I." As if what I want (I yi yi, I can't stop) matters one iota.

Sometimes I wonder if I'm helping these kids. Independent Study doesn't amount to much, but it's better than dropping out. Half of them don't show up for our weekly meeting; they're too busy getting stoned. *Sorry, Miss Johnson, I forgot.* Or working full time, because their parents kicked them out, and they're trying to support themselves. And their babies.

Out of sixteen students, five already have kids. Babies having babies. And on and on. While so many people who desperately want children can't have them. No matter how hard they try. It's enough to make you crazy.

Janessa's having a terrible time with math. She says why does she have to figure stuff out when she can use a calculator? I tell her it's important to understand the concepts. What if there's a worldwide battery shortage? She just looks at me with those big, blank eyes. Anyway, she says, I'm not going to college.

Joe's working more and studying less; his rent eats up most of his salary. He can't go home; his father's made that clear. I've got to find him another book; he can't relate to Shakespeare.

Sam wants to quit so he can work full time; his mother needs more money. Gee, I want to say, has she thought about getting a job? I'd strangle some of these parents if I could ever get them here.

I'm tired tonight. Maybe that's the problem.

I've got to remember to:

1) Test Luis and Carl.
2) Call the JC re: Scott's transcripts.
3) Check with the American Legion re: Sara's scholarship application. We should've heard something by now.
4) Get the custodian to do something about the ants. I realize we're not the biggest school in the district but we're treated like a problem stepchild, a distant relative. The District Office can't spring for a can of bug spray? Is that so much to ask?
5) Buy bigger panty hose.
6) Quit whining.

I met with Raina today. If looks could kill, the ants would be gone and so would I. She talks to me on paper but not in person. She's locked inside herself and won't come out. Toby told me she's homeless; maybe living with her boyfriend? She keeps coming back here. I don't know why. She shows me these beautiful poems she writes, then opens her mouth and blows my mind. She looks like a little girl but she's not. I've got to keep that in mind.

Ricardo says Brenda is carrying a knife. Something about her stepfather. I've got to check that out.

ChAPTER thREE

He was the most beautiful thing she'd ever seen, even now when he was so skinny. She'd watch him sleeping and think: He's mine. His chest was pale and smooth, not hairy, with a tattoo here, and here, on his arm.

They were lying on the floor, legs walking all around them. It was time to get up. The room was cold. She nudged Sonny's shoulder. He woke up foggy, reaching for a smoke, but the pack was empty.

"Cigarette?" she asked somebody passing by. One dropped in her lap. She and Sonny shared it.

Miraculously, the bathroom was empty. The door wouldn't lock, so she held it closed. She rubbed her fingers across a lump of soap and washed her face. Dried it on her sweatshirt.

Someone pounded on the door. "Come on! I gotta go!"

Kimmy came in and flopped on the toilet. It was her apartment and Rita's and Caleb's. "You guys got any money?"

"No," Raina said.

"I'm starving. What time's the Food Pantry open?"

"Don't know." She went there only when she had to; they gave you dirty looks with the day-old bread.

"There's gotta be something around here to eat." Kimmy zipped up and they went into the kitchen, but everyone had scarfed up the crumbs like ants.

Sonny stumbled over to her, holding his head, skinning back his long white hair with his fingers.

"How you feeling, baby?" she asked him, knowing. His face was pinched. They had to do something quick. Every day it got harder to feed Sonny's pet.

He'd been busted several times. Got out right away. Told people his dad had pulled some strings. His father was a bigshot lawyer for the city. She knew he wouldn't even take Sonny's calls. When Sonny was sixteen and still at home, his dad came into his room one night, looked down at him lying in the bed, and said, "I wish you wouldn't wake up tomorrow."

She figured Sonny walked by turning names. He'd be dead if people found out.

Last night they'd sat on the roof and talked. Sonny told her everything was going to change. He always did that as soon as he got high, feeling in control, no muscles screaming. "We gotta quit this stuff and get healthy," he'd said. "Start over. Get jobs and a place of our own."

She knew better than to ask him how. He'd left school in tenth grade but had no trouble getting work; he was so blond and friendly and good-looking. She'd seen pictures. But the jobs never lasted; he'd show up late. He'd oversleep. He'd call in sick. Forget to call. Not show up at all. Come in stoned. Skim money from the till. He needed it, see; he was strung out, hurting.

The years were carved on his face like scars. Wouldn't nobody hire Sonny now.

"You can go to college," he'd said last night, flying. "Get loans or something. You can do it, you're smart."

Usually he thought school was a waste of time. Made fun of her when she wrote in her notebooks. Got ahold of one and read a poem out loud. People laughed, he made it sound so stupid. She tried to grab it back but she was too small. When he finally gave it back she tore it up. He'd ruined it.

On the roof last night he'd talked about their future. Things were gonna change. Sometime real soon. But not this morning, not today; he needed a fix and he needed it now. And he needed new shoes; his were falling apart. Nobody in the place had any money or dope. Everybody started arguing.

Luckily, Stevie Joe dropped by. He was a real nice guy. They called him Robin Hood. When you were broke he'd float you dope to tide you over. He bought groceries and diapers for people's kids. He rode a big Harley and wore black leather and mirrored shades, if it was day or night, like he was starring in the movie about his life and everyone was watching.

He'd brought a box of doughnuts for people to share. Then he and Sonny went into the bathroom. When he came out Sonny was smiling.

"Let's go down to the Plaza." He kissed Raina's cheek. "There's always lots of tourists there on weekends."

She'd tell them she was a runaway and needed a quarter to call her mom. I've changed my mind! she'd sob. I wanna go home! The tourists always gave her more, she looked so young and scared. Sonny waited for her around the corner. Most people were nice, but a few were sharks, cruising for little kids. She could've made lots of money that way. But she and Sonny were engaged.

The other day he'd said something weird. He knew he was asking a lot, A LOT, but couldn't she just do it once in a while? Not with perverts. And nothing strange or dangerous, but just so they'd have some money, honey?

What are you saying? She was shouting, drunk.

Look, he'd do it himself, he explained, but the guys who want to sleep with guys have AIDS, and the guys who sleep with women don't.

ARE YOU SO FUCKING STUPID? OR DO YOU JUST NOT CARE? She socked him. He smacked her. They got in a fight, then things got blurry and they forgot. He hadn't mentioned it again.

Stevie Joe laid out some lines. People crowded close. Someone bumped his elbow. "Watch it, man," he said, frowning. The guy apologized, almost crying. "No worries," Stevie Joe said gently, letting the guy go first, then everyone else. Soon everybody was talking and laughing. Then someone said, "Shit, it's the landlord," an old drunk but he wasn't drunk now.

"You kids gotta get out of here," he said. "Too many people not paying."

"We're paying!" Kimmy shouted. "It's our apartment! We can have friends over if we want to!"

"The neighbors been complaining—"

"You should see what they're doing!" Kimmy's nose holes were ringed with white powder.

"Look at this place. It's a goddamn dump."

11

"It was a dump when we moved in!"

"You listen to me—"

"No, you listen to me!"

She was just showing off. People packed up their stuff, blankets and trash bags full of clothes. Someone asked Stevie Joe could they crash with him. He looked sad and said no. Nobody knew where he lived.

Out on the sidewalk the sun was too bright. Sonny looked bad. She could smell herself. Maybe they could sneak another shower at the health club.

There was a guy at the door now. He said forget it. She could go to the Y, but that was a hassle; they always tried to get her into counseling or the teen shelter when all she wanted was to wash her hair.

They headed downtown, the traffic thick. Sonny did this thing he always did: stepped into the crosswalk, not waiting for the light. People slammed on their brakes so they wouldn't hit him, then hung out their windows, screaming. Sonny grinned.

"That's so stupid," she said.

"No worries," he told her. He believed that he had some kind of good luck. So why were they sleeping in boarded-up buildings, in unlocked cars, on people's floors? So many people crammed into the apartments, you didn't know whose it was, but it didn't matter; they took care of each other. And ripped each other off. She'd done it herself, taken clothes and stuff. She had to; there wasn't any money. She tried to get jobs, but people looked at her like she and Sonny were wearing matching sweatshirts that said I'M WITH THE JUNKIE. And when she did get work, some jerk got in her face and she had to tell them off.

She wasn't a little kid anymore. She wasn't taking shit from anyone.

The main thing she had to do was stay in school. She couldn't say why that was important. Maybe because Sonny and her friends thought it was stupid. She didn't like doing what people wanted. Didn't want anyone thinking they knew her, thinking they had a map to her mind. School was the place where Miss Johnson waited, telling her: *Raina, this is a wonderful story. You should submit it to a literary journal. Maybe the—*

She'd cut off the teacher: "Does it pay?"

Well, no, but—

Screw it. She'd walk away, the praise a burning nugget in her heart.

The tourists weren't biting. The weather was too good. People felt sorrier for them when it rained.

"Fucking tightwads." Stevie Joe's treat had worn off, and Sonny's hands were shaking. They walked down to Macy's. He waited outside. She could steal some stuff, then try to return it. That worked sometimes, but probably not today; today she looked too dirty.

She rode the escalator up to the ladies' lounge. Washed her hands for a while. The soap smelled good. Women came and went, some with babies in strollers, some with big white bags full of purchases. Raina rummaged in her pockets like she was hunting for something. Her timing had to be perfect.

The lounge door opened. An old lady came in, followed by a couple of younger women. The old lady was wrinkled but she was wearing a suit, and big rings sparkled on her fingers.

She took the last stall at the end of the row. The young women took stalls beside each other. Laughing and talking, they finished their business, then washed their hands and put on lipstick.

At the end of the row the old lady sat frozen, her handbag between her feet.

The young women left the lounge, the door closing behind them. The room was silent. Raina sat real still. She could feel the old lady waiting, listening, until she thought she was alone and no one would hear her go.

The next thing she knows, a girl's head's under the door. They stared at each other, not saying a word. Raina snatched the purse and was back on the street while the old lady was still struggling with her girdle.

At the park she and Sonny sat on a bench and dumped everything out of the purse: Kleenex, lipstick, dental floss, credit cards—they'd have to use those quick—keys, a gold pen, family pictures, a comb, and seventy-five bucks and change.

They tossed the junk in a trash can, then hit some stores and charged everything they could carry: clothes, watches, sleeping bags, toothpaste, shampoo, cigarettes, expensive candy, then treated themselves to Chinese food for lunch.

They traded cash and a credit card for Sonny's meds, some crank for her, and a bottle of booze at a place where the guy never asked any questions, never even looked into their faces.

At a hotel where they stayed when they had the dough they tried to make love, then Sonny fell asleep, his arms flung back against the sheets like someone was holding a gun on him.

Raina stood in the shower for a real long time, shampooing her hair until it squeaked.

Daylight faded from the windows. Sonny snored beside her. Raina drained the vodka bottle and watched TV, scribbling in her notebook until she fell asleep, still clutching the old lady's gold pen.

And woke up the next morning thinking: We forgot to get Sonny any shoes.

CHAPTER FOUR

I don't know why my mother hates me. Maybe she hated my father more than the others. I didn't like him either. Luckily, he wasn't around for long. Men came and went, most of them mean, leaving behind: Raymond, Sheila, Lynette, Lorraine, Willie, Bobby and Brandy. Seven children and she never wanted one.

Especially me.

Not that she babied the others. Once, she hit Raymond twenty times. I counted. And she'd get right in Sheila's face and scream so hard, her veins stuck out like Frankenstein's. You think you got it bad? You shoulda seen my childhood! As if somehow it was Sheila's fault. The way my mother sees it, she's been robbed, ever since she was a tiny girl. What she didn't get then, she's going to get now.

My mother's the only child in her world.

I called Sheila a few weeks ago. She'd left messages around. It had been, oh God, a year since we'd talked.

Even though we all live in the same city, we're not what you'd call a close family.

She skipped the how-you-been stuff and went straight to the point. Sheila and I don't get along.

"Mom wanted me to call you."

"Why? What's wrong?"

"Nothing. She wants us to be on TV."

"What?"

"Just listen. You know the Larry Singer show?"

"No." My hectic schedule doesn't allow for much TV.

"He's this talk show host. People get on and talk about their problems and their families."

"So?"

"He wants our family to be on the show."

"How's he know about us?"

"She called him. There's a number at the end, and you call the show. They're gonna be in the city interviewing people."

"What's this got to do with me?"

"You're part of the family." Sheila sounded pissed. "They want everybody there so it'll be more real."

"Maybe we could all get in a fight."

"Look, it wasn't my idea to call you! Mom wants to get on. It's the least you can do."

"Right. After everything she's done for me."

I could hear Sheila smoking, blowing hard.

I said, "Will Willie be there?"

"Maybe. He's in juvie."

"What about Ray and Lynette?"

"Ray's in jail."

"For what?"

"Being stupid. Selling crank to a cop. Lyn's back East."

17

"How come?"

"She and Gary finally got married."

"How's Brandy doing?"

"You can ask her yourself. Don't you wanna be on TV?"

"Not really."

"Mom wants you there! The people said—"

How many times can you trick a dog into coming back so you can kick him? A lot. A lot. This time you might pet him.

So I called the number Sheila gave me and made an appointment to "audition." That's why I didn't show up at school that week. One reason.

The appointment was in this big hotel downtown. The doorman tried to chase me off until I said who I was meeting.

I rode the elevator to the top of the building, up to the penthouse, one whole floor. A guy opened the door, looking too glad to see me. Another guy was on the phone the whole time I was there.

"Lorraine? Come in! Dick Simpson! Associate producer. We've heard so much about you!"

"I'll bet."

"Sit down! Can I get you something to drink?"

"Yeah, a fifth of vodka."

"Ha-ha! Seriously, would you like a soda?"

I was playing the part, being who he expected. I didn't want to disappoint him. Or her.

"So!" Dick said. "They tell me you're homeless. That must be pretty rough."

"Yeah." The place was huge, with a thick white carpet and a glass wall framing the skyline and bridge. The furniture was all chrome and leather. "That wig sure looks real," I said.

"It is." He looked alarmed.

"Real hair cost more?"

"No, I mean it's mine. See?" He didn't look happy. "So, anyway," he said, "you left home when you were twelve."

"For good? Or all the other times she kicked me out?"

"For good, I guess."

"Fourteen." I lit a Marlboro.

"Your mom said you two don't get along. Is that right?" He handed me a gold and crystal bowl for an ashtray.

"You're kidding me," the other guy said into the phone.

"She said you were incorrigible," Dick added.

"I doubt it. She wouldn't even know what that means."

"Uncontrollable, she meant."

"She said that?"

"Not exactly." His eyes bulged. "I gathered that you were the most difficult of all her children."

"Most intelligent," I said. "She don't like that."

"Why not? Please tell me about it, Lorraine." He leaned forward, lips parted for a juicy morsel.

I acted like I was trying not to cry. Was this my cue for tears? Not yet.

I said, "Wouldn't it be better for me to answer on TV, to keep it, you know, spontaneous and fresh?"

"Well, yes, but—that's a very good point, Lorraine. But we need to know what kind of dialogue might develop, especially since the show is live."

"Live?"

"Scary, right?" He winked at me. "But it sure gives us an edge in the ratings."

"Because there's no telling what might happen."

"Exactly. But I don't want you to think that's what Larry's all about. What he's trying to do is open the lines of communication. Bring people together. Solve problems. Help the family. Because without the family unit, what've you got, Lorraine?"

"My life."

"Ha-ha!" he said. "You've seen the show?"

"No."

"We've got a trained psycholgist. I mean a real one; not one of these nuts who's plugging a book. She helps put the family back together."

"After the show?"

"No, in the last fifteen minutes. Then Larry comes on and gives his parting shot— Let me run one for you, give you some idea."

He put a videotape into the VCR. A pack of wackos screamed at each other while the studio audience hooted and hollered, egged on by the host, who gazed into the camera, shaking his head in sorrow.

"See what I mean, how Larry draws them out?"

My mind drifted away. I wished Sonny were there. The penthouse looked like he pictures heaven: enormous and white. Rooms full of clean beds.

"You're not listening, you bitch!" someone shrieked on the TV. That's what people really want: attention. My mother craves the big fix: an audience applauding her, and somebody famous calling her by name: *So tell us, Carla . . .* millions of listeners, hearing how bad her life has been, then leaping to their feet for a standing ovation, shouting: *You're right, Carla: You were gypped. So now it will always be your turn.*

20

"Okay, you get the idea. Jeez, those people were screamers." Dick turned off the VCR. "What happens is, Larry will ask you some questions based on the information we've been given. Your mother said something"-he glanced through a notepad on the coffee table-"about foster homes. Detention homes. Can't read my own damn scribbling. You were in foster homes?"

"Yeah."

"How many?"

"A million."

"Why?"

"Ask my mother. She put me there."

"All right. That's good. What we're looking for, Lorraine, is human emotion. Real people. Real pain. Don't hold anything back. If you feel it, say it. It's okay if you swear. We can bleep that. Get it off your chest! Get it out! There's always two sides to every story, am I right? Honest communication. That's what we're after. That's the only way the healing process can begin. Besides, it makes for dynamite television. Your mother tells us you're a junkie."

The guy on the phone said, "No, not really. What makes you think so, Fred?"

I couldn't believe it. "She said that?"

"Would you be willing to admit it on the show? We'll disguise you if you want; a wig, dark glasses-"

"Would I have to show my tracks?"

"Needle marks? No. Unless you want to," he added eagerly.

"The ones in my ears might not show up good on camera."

"In your ears? Don't you use your arms?"

"There's some on my tongue, too. See?" I stuck it out.

"They're too small, I guess."

I almost laughed in his face but I was hurting. Telling him I'm a goddamn junkie when I've never touched a needle in my life. She's the one.

"She tell you she's a shooter?"

"What, guns?" He looked confused.

"Meth. Speed. And she snorts and takes pills. But she don't do weed. You gotta draw the line somewhere."

"I don't believe she mentioned that." Dick wrote on his notepad. "Your sister Sheila says you're an alcoholic."

"She should know. Did she mention the time she and that girl got in a fight, and the cops—"

"Your mother seems to think"—he was grazing through his notes—"that your substance abuse problem has something to do with Bobby."

I lit up a smoke. "I ain't talking about Bobby."

"He was the baby of the family, wasn't he?"

"You heard what I said. I ain't talking about Bobby."

He placed a cold hand on my arm. "Wouldn't it be better to get it out, Lorraine? After all, it wasn't your fault. When he died you were only, what, seven years old."

I laughed. Oh, what that laugh cost me.

Then I spoke to him in a different voice. The one I use here, with you.

"She'll say anything to get on this show. It's her favorite, you know. She never misses it."

"What do you mean?" He quit patting my arm. "Are you saying this isn't for real?"

I shrugged.

"All the stuff your mother said, the stories she told me—"

"Her doctor says it's best to play along. We don't want her having another breakdown."

22

"Good God."

"She probably won't. She's on medication. But you might want to check with your TV shrink."

"Well, talk to the attorneys," said the man on the phone. "Our asses are blowing in the breeze here."

"This probably happens to you a lot," I said. "Can we still be on Larry's show?"

"So you're not a homeless junkie?"

"Nope."

He groaned, the enormity of this near disaster sinking in.

"Hey," I said, "I have an idea for the show. You know what would be killer for the ratings?"

"What?" He leaned toward me again, his eyes greedy.

"Have somebody pick off a big ugly scab. Just peel it right off. Or stab a kitten. The camera zooms in. All this blood and guts. Or somebody could die on the show. Before your eyes. Some old guy with cancer. Or a kid in a coma and his brain's not working. He could be unplugged. His whole family sobbing. And the TV viewers could be right there, and it'd be so sad, they'd almost feel something—"

"Whoever you are, get out," Dick said.

As a consolation prize, I took the ashtray with me.

By the time I called my mother she'd heard from the show. Thanks, they'd said, but no. Would she like free tickets?

"You really fucked up big time!" she shouted. "Couldn't you do this one thing for me?"

"You lied about Bobby!"

"You're the liar!" she said. "A liar your whole life!"

"That's not true, and you know it! You know what you done! You're the one, not me!"

Then we said a bunch of stuff, and she hung up.

Too bad I didn't pass the audition. Things might've changed, might've turned out different. Maybe the TV shrink could've helped us. Maybe all the hurts would've been forgiven. Maybe we finally would've been a real family.

It would've made for dynamite television.

CHAPTER FIVE

Dear Superintendent Kelley,

Remember me? Margaret Johnson, the teacher at Emmanuel Wright Continuation High? The school that looks like a public restroom with flags?

I just wanted to let you know that you can stop worrying about the ants. They're not a problem anymore. They're gone. They drowned. The leaks in the roof are beyond belief. Learning to swim has become a graduation requirement.

Superintendent Kelley, I'd like to know why you're building a band room at Doris Washington, and approved thirty (thirty!) new computers for Hiram Clawson, when at EWC we're up to our necks in trash cans full of asbestos dust and water.

By the way, the new trash cans are lovely. Thank you.

You talk about The Importance of Education, and Investing in Our Most Precious Resource, Our Youth, yet you write off my kids like a bad debt. Problem children. Too much trouble. Maybe that's why you sent over the trash cans. So we can haul them to the dump.

All these kids need is a chance to succeed and adults they can count on. We can spend the money now on education or we will surely spend it later: on welfare, probation officers, drug rehab, crack babies.

I wish I had the guts to say this.

Sam quit. He took that sheet metal job. I begged his mother to let him finish the year. He was so close to graduating.

She said, "He can always get his GED. Right now we need the money."

He'd gotten Social Security since he was seven, when his dad died. Then he turned eighteen and they cut him off. His mother was used to that steady income; she insisted he take the job. "We all have to grow up sometime," she said. He's such a nice kid. I'll miss him.

Sara's applied to UC Berkeley. Even though she's POSITIVE she won't get in, because who wants people with a juvenile record? Anyway, she says, she doesn't have the money. That's what loans and scholarships are for. I tell her she's got a really good chance; if not at Berkeley, maybe at Chico or Davis. She wants to believe me but she's afraid; why hope for something and get disappointed?

Brenda said Ricardo's wrong; she isn't carrying a knife, and if he doesn't shut his mouth, she'll stick him.

New kid this week. Not sure what to make of him. Thomas from L.A., staying with his dad. His mother kicked him out. He goes back and forth. Looks at me with these tired eyes like he's seen it all before.

I tried to talk to Raina today. I asked where she's been

staying. She wouldn't tell me, of course. She writes down all this personal stuff, then, when I act concerned, she backs off. All she wants to know is, is the writing any good? Yes, it's her story that's appalling.

I said: You must've felt terrible when Bobby died. Duh. She stared at me, her eyes so cold. It sounds like, duh, something terrible happened. Trying to give her an opening, a door. She slammed it in my face.

Her writing is so articulate and insightful that it's hard to believe it comes out of the same kid who acts so rude and tough. Interrupting when I'm working with Scott, then telling him to shut up. Raina, that's uncalled for, I said. You'll have to wait your turn.

Forget it. Help the idiot. She slammed out the door, stopping to light a cigarette and toss the match on the floor.

Scott, I said, I apologize. I don't approve of that kind of language.

That's okay, Miss Johnson, he said. The bitch don't know any better.

I have got to buy bigger panty hose. I'll need the Jaws of Life to get these off.

I intended to get some at Payless today when I stopped to buy supplies for school; exotic stuff, like pencils and paper. By the time they arrive from the District Office, the kids will have quit or graduated.

But on my way toward the panty hose aisle I passed a display of pregnancy tests, those little boxes with the hopeful names: Answer, Promise, Tomorrow.

I used to love to buy them, to follow the directions, counting the minutes while the future developed, our son or daughter, there, on paper. Then flying to the phone to call my husband at work. Sid would always come home with flowers and champagne. . . .

But the baby that was coming always slipped away; disappeared without a trace. No heartbeat, no pictures. As if it were just a dream we'd shared, so real we woke up in tears.

After a while we couldn't look at each other, our faces reflecting only pain.

I almost died when Sid sent me the picture of his twins, then despised myself for feeling jealous. Those are not your babies, I told myself. Your children are safe in your heart. They will never feel pain. They will never grow old. This world can never hurt them.

But why is it so hard for some people to have kids when thousands who don't want them give birth every day? Like that cheerleader who delivered her baby in the bathroom, then went back to the football game. Why can't we trade?

I tried and tried. How can those days be done? So irrevocably. So suddenly.

I saw that display of pregnancy tests and stood there for a moment, then my mind went somewhere else. When I came to, I was driving home, crying. Kind of the way I was thirty one day, and the next, I was forty-five.

CHAPTER SIX

The weather turned bad, and she lost her coat. Sonny didn't feel cold; he was always flying. Every dime they could get went into his neck. The veins in his arms had collapsed, exhausted.

She was hungry all the time.

Grabbed handfuls of mints and flavored toothpicks at Sizzler. Swiped fruit from the bins outside the Chinaman's store. Boosted what she could at Safeway: not much—private pigs pretended to be shoppers. Lifted purses left behind in shopping carts while their owners, so stupid, wandered down the aisle. Stole change cans: UNICEF, Save the Children. Grabbed a pizza and ran out the door while the people who'd paid were on their way to the counter. Or called in an order that would be tossed out later when nobody picked it up. One place wouldn't play: they sprayed their Dumpster with ammonia. She and Sonny smashed a window, someone shouting inside.

Stood with the winos and the losers and the dying in

the long lines outside the soup kitchen.

"Look," Sonny said, his face twitching, "that teacher will give you money. She likes you. You gotta ask her. Are you listening to me?"

But she wasn't asking no one for nothing.

At night they slept in the Laundromat. Old Bert the wino watchman liked them, even though they'd stolen some clothes one time. He let them lean against the warm dryers. The place was filthy but it had a bathroom with a sink; cold water, no mirror. Bert said if there was a mirror, people hung around. He tried to remember to keep it locked when he was gone or people were in there doing God knows what. I can't let no one sleep here, he explained; if the boss finds out, I'll lose my job. But he pretended not to notice when she and Sonny conked out, curled beneath an old Bekins blanket.

"Let's hit the park," Sonny said when they woke up. She washed her face and combed her hair with her fingers. She made him wash his face. He needed a shave. Bert gave them a few bucks to get something to eat and promised he'd bring Sonny a razor. They ate doughnuts on their way downtown.

One way they got money was by hitting up the punks who drove to the city every weekend so they could hang out with people like Sonny and Raina, pretending to be hardcore. Rich high school kids who liked to act poor. Posers, Sonny called them, not to their faces.

When they got near the park, he made sure the posers saw him. Then he plunged into the crosswalk, against the light.

A truck screeched to a stop, inches from his thigh. The

driver's purple face screamed, "Do you want to get killed?"

"That'd be tough on your insurance." The posers laughed with him, trying to look cool in their warm leather coats, faces painted white as fluorescent lights, spider eyes, hair dyed purple green yellow, tongue studs, ear cuffs, braces on their teeth.

The wind rattled the Christmas lights strung high above the park. Raina could not stop shivering.

The posers bought them lattes and fancy pastries, and gave them boxes of imported cigarettes. They played CDs of bands Raina and Sonny had never heard of, and talked about drugs and anarchy and the high cost of concert tickets.

A kid named Jason had his arm around Sonny. He was tall and blond and pretty. Sonny looked like his ghost. Jason liked people to see him laughing; to know he was having the most fun, the best dope. Gold chains and hippie shit were tangled at his throat. The big diamond stud in his ear was real.

Sonny laughed at Jason's jokes, but she knew he was thinking: Come on! Let's go! He needed a shot. He'd find the dope, then Jason bought and gave Sonny some, on commission, he said. Jason said his habit was no big deal; he just liked a taste of the real stuff now and then. Liked acting big and bad. Amaze your friends. He wanted to hang around and bullshit, but Sonny was in a hurry.

She followed them when they left the park with a girl named Wally, who looked like she'd drowned, and a boy named Gary, dressed in black with a diaper pin stuck through his eyebrow.

Sonny had forgotten all about her. He never even turned around.

Tourists melted back to let them pass. They entered an alley. Tall buildings blocked the sun. The wind was fierce, but Sonny was sweating in his thin white shirt with all the buttons gone.

"You guys wait here," he said. "I'll be right back."

Jason looked startled. "Why? Where you going?"

"On a cruise to Alaska. Where you think?"

"We've never done it like this before," Jason said.

"That's how my man wants it. You got the dough?"

"Well, yeah, but—"

"What's the matter, don't you trust me?" Sonny was puffing one of Jason's cigarettes. "If you don't trust me, man—"

"No, I do, it's not that."

"So what's the problem?" Sonny sounded bored.

"No problem," Jason said. His friends looked embarrassed. "It's just, you know, he always meets us here."

"Things change," Sonny said. "Do you want to deal or don't you?"

Jason looked unhappy. He said, "Yeah."

"I'll be right back. Raina'll stay here with you."

"What?"

"You heard me. You baby-sit."

Jason pulled out his wallet and took out the money. But the way Sonny reached for it made everything change. In that split second he looked too naked, too hungry. Raina saw Jason seeing the matted hair, the lips caked with spit, the bony wrists—

Jason put the wallet back into his pocket. "Fucking junkie," he said. "Get out of my way."

Tears filled Sonny's eyes. Then he was lying on Jason, holding a knife to his throat.

"Jesus Christ!" Wally cried. "What're you doing? Don't hurt him!"

Gary went off like a car alarm.

"You two better shut up," Sonny said. "Unless you want your friend talking out of his neck. You can smoke like that too. I seen a guy do it. His voice kinda sounded like Daffy Duck."

"This is stupid." Raina reached into Wally's satchel for matches and a cigarette, lit one up.

"I'll tell you what's stupid!" Sonny's face was an inch from Jason's. "You and your friends come around here playing games, then you get tired and go home to Mom and Dad. This isn't a game, man! This is real! How do you like it?"

Jason was crying.

"Now what?" Raina said.

Sonny looked at Wally and said, "Give her the jacket."

"The what?"

"You heard me. Give her the goddamn coat!"

Wally took it off, trembling, and handed it to Raina.

"Don't worry, Daddy'll buy you another one," Sonny said. "Try it on, baby. How's it fit?"

"It's kinda big."

"This ain't Macy's. You too," he told Gary.

Fumbling with the buttons, Gary stripped off his coat and dropped it on the ground near Raina's feet.

"You guys oughta thank me," Sonny said. "Consider this an education." He pulled out Jason's wallet and tossed it to Raina. "You know what they say, kids: Drugs are bad."

He sliced off the gold chains; the hippie beads scattered. Then he leaned close enough to kiss Jason's ear and plucked out the diamond with his teeth.

Jason whimpered and moaned. Sonny got to his feet. "Get out of here," he said.

They ran down the alley.

Sonny put on Gary's coat and tucked the diamond in his pocket. "Shit!" he said suddenly, smacking his head. "I shoulda took his shoes. They woulda fit me."

"You stupid asshole!"

"Don't worry, I'll buy some."

"You were gonna take the money and split!"

"Are you nuts?"

"Leave me with those kids!" she screamed. "You god-damn greedy junkie!"

"Don't say that. I love you."

"Fucking liar!" She hit him.

He slapped her. She slugged him until he held her tight. "You were gonna leave me, you asshole, you junkie."

They hugged each other, crying. He kissed the top of her head and said, "I guess we'll never know."

CHAPTER SEVEN

Once upon a time there was a girl named Bug Brains.
Teacher said: Children, it's not her fault.
They called her names because she was dirty.
How's a little kid supposed to wash her clothes?

Teacher sent home a note for her mother,
but the little girl's mother was not at home.
Her brothers came back. She told them what happened.
They laughed and said: Don't use my comb.

She looked and looked at herself in the mirror
She couldn't see nothing wrong.
fell asleep that night waiting for her mother
but the mother did not come home.

When the girl woke up the house was empty.
found clothes on the floor and put them on.
But the teacher had told her: You can't come back
until your little problem's gone.

She waited and waited and waited and waited
but the mother did not come home.

She had to get to school! Didn't have any money,
so she went to a store and stole special shampoo.
The people caught her. They called her mother.
Who finally came. Said: What'd you do?

They told her what happened. She got real mad
and grabbed the girl and pinched her skin
and shouted at her: I'll beat your butt!
And when they got home that's what she did.

Then the mother felt very guilty.

She washed the girl's clothes and her blankets and sheets.
She washed the girl's hair with special shampoo.
The girl went to school feeling happy and clean
but the kids called her Bug Brains until she moved.

You'd think someone would've asked a few questions,
like: Why did you leave this kid alone? Why is she always
dirty? Who's the mean-looking guy with the weasel eyes?
Where'd she get all these bruises?

Granny would've cried. For herself and the child,
busted for lice, at the age of eight.

My mother's first bust, but not her last.

I have described my mother as an evil dwarf. The
Wicked Witch of the North. This is not accurate. Beside
her senior yearbook picture it doesn't say: Plans to
marry a succession of pedophiles and losers. Hopes to
have seven children and make them miserable. Career
goal: dead-end jobs at minimum wage.

The words she would've chosen would've read: Hard-working Carla will attend a four-year college. She'll make her first million before she's thirty, be happily married, and have two children.

If there had been a senior picture. She got pregnant with Ray and dropped out.

When they argue, Granny says, I didn't want you to quit. You could've had an abortion or let the baby be adopted.

Liar! my mother shouts; you said I had to keep it! Or were you always so drunk, you don't remember?

They rehash the past as if it were a case they were pleading before the highest court.

There's not much evidence from my mother's childhood; Granny didn't save stuff like photographs or school papers. There were too many kids, too many moves, no camera. Only one picture I used to study, my mother at ten, in a plaid school dress; her bangs haphazard, her face so solemn, you'd think she'd seen what was lying ahead.

Granny says she was a smart girl. The teachers loved her. Did well in school. Made the honors list. But then she changed, for no reason, she—

Liar! You knew what he was doing to me! You let him!

No, Granny insists. You never told me.

I did! You called me a slut, remember?

On and on, the facts as hazy as the smoke from their cigarettes. Granny lives downtown in a studio apartment. She takes the bus to my mother's. They play cards together. The past is a scab they can't leave alone.

"She loves you, Raina. It's just hard for her to show it."

Granny's treating me to lunch downtown, at a hamburger stand open to the street. We're supposed to be talking about my life and figuring out how to fix it.

"See, the problem was my second husband," she explains. "He and the kids didn't get along."

He beat them bloody, according to my mother. The belt buckle cut them.

"So I married Fred."

Who turned out, to no one's surprise but hers, to be another child molester. She thought she couldn't live without a man; that a bad one was better than none.

"Which turned out to be a big mistake," Granny adds. As if I don't know how this story ends. "By the time I knew what was going on, it was too late."

For Granny and my mother. For my mother and me.

"Your mother doesn't understand," she says. Her cheeks are wrinkled. She's only fifty. People stream past; they look like Granny, old faces with the eyes of frightened children. "Well, I've gotta get back to work, honey. If I'm late, the boss'll kill me."

She kisses my cheek and gives me ten bucks.

Who was the monster: my mother or Granny?

I remember happy times, my mother laughing. Or maybe that was a show on TV. A show about a family with lots of kids. Too many kids. You kids shut up. Too many men. Lock the door, Daddy's drunk! Fists punching through the wood. Don't hit my mother! Cops coming. Blood streaming from my mother's nose.

When the welfare check came at the first of the month we'd beg her, Mom, please pay the rent. Pay the rent. They're gonna kick us out. Buy food, Mom. Please. Sometimes she listened, sometimes she didn't, because she'd found a way to make the problems disappear. Fairy dust, white powder, gobbled up her problems. Had her laughing in the kitchen, tossing Bobby in the air. Watch the baby, Granny said. Gobbled up all the money until the problems got so huge, they filled the house and crashed through the roof and the rain came in.

She always found another place. She was dealing by then, bringing in two, three thousand a week. When she wasn't in jail. Or scraping by on food stamps. Or making hash pipes with her girlfriends in the kitchen while the kids ate Sugar Smacks out of the box and the milk was gone so the babies drank Kool-Aid.

One time I asked her: Did you use when you were pregnant with me?

Cigarette smoke curled out of her nose. Obviously, she said.

I spy on her sometimes, trapped behind a checkout line at Kmart, in that ugly jacket with a badge that says HELLO, I'M CARLA! HOW CAN I HELP YOU?; ringing up things on a cash register with a sign that reminds her to GREET SMILE THANK.

She looks so beaten. She used to seem big. She used to be a kid, someone like me. A long time ago. She wanted life to be different. Then Bobby died, but that's another story.

CHAPTER EIGHT

The computers finally arrived. No printers. No software. Am I supposed to create my own? On the phone half the day with the District Office, Juan and Jackie listening at their desks, grinning. Yes, Doris, the new computers came, but— no, I've already looked in the boxes. That's what I'm telling you: without the programs. So we can't, they're just blank— what's taking so long? Is Santa going to deliver them?

Sara's essay didn't win the VFW contest. The commander (Commandant?) said they didn't care for the topic she'd chosen, but I think they were scared because she sounds so smart. Not a kid who'll pledge allegiance without knowing what the words mean. That and the nose ring finished her off.

She said, I knew I wouldn't get it. I told you, Miss Johnson.

Half the time they're right and I'm wrong.

Met with Thomas from L.A. and his father. There's a role model. In the middle of our conference he asked me for a date. Thomas just sitting there, staring at the floor.

I thought I must've heard wrong, so I kept talking and the father says, No, I'm serious, flashing what he thinks is a winning smile. Shit, Thomas says, and he's out the door. He'll be heading down south before long.

Wendy called last night. She's coming for the weekend, maybe after Thanksgiving. It will be so good to talk to another adult. The kids look at me like I'M the child; smiling and shaking their heads while I'm talking, like: You're really nice, Miss Johnson, but you don't have a clue.

Maybe I should teach in private school. It would be great to have that much parent support. Wendy said that when St. Peter's had their open house, NINETY PERCENT of the parents came. For public schools to get that kind of turnout we'd have to offer free doughnuts and an open bar.

I don't want to give up, but I feel so discouraged.

I shouldn't think about this when I'm tired.

The situation with Raina is bizarre. She came in late for our appointment this morning, filthy, smelling of booze and cigarettes, and handed me these wrinkled binder pages, wanting me to read them right now. Right now! Nothing else matters; not math, not her test scores. Watching me read, trying to see what I'm thinking. Then, when I say, this is wonderful, Raina, she acts like: Who cares, it's just a stupid poem, just another stupid story about her family.

Anyway, she said, who'd want to read it? Nobody'd pay me for stuff like that.

Sometimes what you write is just for you, I said. To figure out what you're thinking.

She crumpled up the pages real big and noisy. But she put them in her pocket, not the trash.

"Raina, we've got to talk," I said.

"About what?"

41

"Your life."

She shrugged. "Nothing to say."

"Apparently there's plenty. Where are you staying?"

"At the Hilton."

"Can't we be friends, Raina?"

"No."

"Come on, you can give it to me straight."

She almost smiled. Her fingernails are bitten down to blood. Like mine.

"You can't smoke in here."

She flicked ashes on the floor. The ideal moment for the Superintendent to drop by, as he's promised to so many times.

"There are people who can help you, Raina."

"I don't need help."

"They'll take care of you and give you a place to stay."

"I take care of myself."

"There's the Children's Shelter."

"I ain't no child."

"And the foster program—"

She scraped back her chair.

"I know you want help. That's why you show me your writing."

"I'm making up stories. That's all," she said.

"Can't you be honest with yourself, Raina? I know you want to tell me what happened to Bobby. That's why you keep writing about him."

"That ain't why."

"If you can't say it, why not put it down on paper? It'll just be between the two of us, I promise."

But I'd gone too far. I'd pushed too hard.

Without another word she was out the door.

CHAPTER NINE

One of Sonny's teeth was hurting but he wouldn't go to the free clinic. He said the tooth wasn't the problem; it was her: she drank up all the money. He reeled around, slurring.

"Real funny," she said, trying to ignore him. They were huddled in a store doorway, out of the wind.

Sonny's face got ugly. "You acted disgusting, throwing up in front of all those people. Shit."

She could've said bunch of junkies, who cares. But the best thing to do was keep her mouth shut.

"They were gonna let us stay till you fucked up. I'm serious," he said. "You got a real problem, Raina."

She could've said: Tell the guy in the mirror. When she met him his habit was a tiny little pet, but now it was a horse that rode him.

"You hear what I'm saying? The truth hurts, don't it. Why don't you say something?"

She wouldn't, so he shoved her. They pushed each other against the windows until somebody came out and said I'm calling the cops. She walked off.

"Nice going," Sonny said to her back.

He needed a fix and they were dead broke, so they looked all around but couldn't find Stevie Joe. They went down to the Plaza but the day was cold; the tourists kept their hands in their pockets. Hey, man, Sonny said, it's the Christmas season. The season for giving, you tight-wad bastards.

She went to Macy's to get some stuff to return or maybe snag a purse if she got lucky, but a rent-a-cop grabbed her and threw her out. She and Sonny had burned too many places. People knew their faces and drove them off like dogs.

Maybe they could borrow some money from Bert. When they got to the Laundromat he wasn't around. A guy in camouflage was reading a *Watchtower* while his clothes dried.

"How's the war going, Sarge?"

The guy looked at Sonny.

"Who's winning, us or them?"

The guy just stared.

"Mind if we bum one of those cigarettes?"

"Yeah." The guy didn't blink. His eyes were scary.

"We're starving, man. How 'bout you loan us a dollar? Come on, fifty cents."

"Let's go," Raina said.

"Fifty cents, man. That's all I'm asking. A quarter. A dime."

She tugged Sonny's sleeve.

"A nickel. A penny. Hey, we pay you, Sarge!"

She grabbed Sonny's arm, pulled him out the door.

"What's the matter with you?" she said. "He's nuts."

"So what?" Sonny said. "These goddamn shoes."

"You shoulda got some when we had the money."

"You drink it all up."

"You're a goddamn liar."

"Don't call me a liar."

"Who's the junkie? Not me."

He grabbed her and slammed her against a building. Then his eyes got sad and he kissed her mouth as if he were trying to hide inside her. She tasted tears. They hugged each other hard.

They passed an antique store with stuff out front. Raina sat down in a wooden wheelchair, and Sonny wheeled it off. The owner ran out and squawked, but Sonny snarled at him and he went back inside.

They parked near the Plaza. It worked out great: the tourists gave her money and asked about her legs. She said there was hope, maybe an operation. Then they saw a cop and left the chair behind.

Sonny wanted to get high, but Raina said no; they had to eat first, did he want to get sick? She wouldn't give him the money. They gulped down corn dogs. Let's go, let's go! He was on a mission.

The streets were deserted. They couldn't find anybody but the skeleton guy nobody liked to deal with; the skin on his face so tight he always smiled. No, Sonny, she said, don't use that needle. Just wait—too late. He was smiling too.

"Things are gonna get better. They're gonna be different. Are you listening to me, baby?"

"Sure," she said, smoking a cigarette, trying to look interested, but freezing on the park bench. "Let's go see Bert." Hearing in her mind the warm roar of the dryers.

Nah, Sonny said, he wanted to party. They went by Kimmy's, but she'd moved out and the people wouldn't let them in.

"Shit," Sonny said. He was coming down quick. "That asshole burned me."

"What'd you expect?"

"I'll kill that bastard! I'll tear him apart! I've got more muscle in my shit than he's got in his whole body!"

They couldn't find the guy. They couldn't find anybody.

"Jesus Christ," Sonny howled, "where'd everyone go?"

"To Florida for the winter."

"Whose side are you on?" As if he were playing a game he could win.

She followed as he raged up and down the sidewalks, fixed on revenge, his body quivering. After a while he forgot about the guy. He had to get high.

"We got any money left?"

"Not enough," she said.

"We gotta get some money right now! I'm in trouble!"

She saw his face change. She knew what was coming.

"One guy. Just this once," he said. "That's all I'm asking."

"Fuck you." She turned away, but he grabbed her arms.

"I need it, Raina!"

"Let go."

"Don't you love me?"

"You're hurting me, you asshole!"

"Listen, baby. Honey, please. I'll never ask you again. I swear. I promise. But this is an emergency! I'm really sick."

"Then go to the Clinic."

"I will, tomorrow morning. First thing I'm gonna do. Get offa this shit."

"You must think I'm so stupid."

"I need you, baby. I love you so much." He cupped her face. "Just this once. I promise."

"But I love you, Sonny." Crying like a baby. "We're supposed to be engaged."

"We're still engaged. I'm gonna marry you, honey. That's why it's so beautiful you'd do this for me."

He pressed her to his chest. She could feel his heart beating.

"Let's go find Bert," she said. "He'll give us some money."

Sonny turned her face to the busy street. "Look around you, honey. We're alone on the planet. It's you and me, baby. That's all we've got."

"But I want things to be the way they used to be."

"They will! I promise. We'll sit on the hill and watch the boats come in, all the little sailboats on the bay. Go skating at the rink, with all the lights twinkling and the music playing. Wouldn't you like that, honey? I just need you to do this one little thing. Just sex, that's all it is. It don't mean nothing. I'm gonna marry you, honey. And I'm gonna get clean. I'm so sick of this shit. I mean it, I've had it. Things are gonna change. Real soon, I promise. Look at me, Raina. You believe me, don't you, honey?"

His eyes were so sad, she had to look away. "I don't wanna get in anybody's car," she whispered.

"You can take him to the hotel. I'll be right outside the room." He kissed her face softly again and again.

"Don't worry, honey. Nothing weird's gonna happen. I'd kill anybody who hurt you."

They started toward the block where people shopped for bodies. Fog was rolling down the street. Sonny walked fast. It was hard to keep up. He pushed through the crowds, his torn sneakers flapping.

"We gotta get you some shoes," she told his back.

He turned around and smiled, feeling so much better already, he didn't wait for the light at the corner to change. He jumped off the curb and into the crosswalk, hungry for the thrill of screeching tires, the shrill joy of forcing people not to kill him—in front of a car driven by someone just like him, another kid who didn't give a damn.

And went sailing through the air until he hit the pavement, his head splashing open like a water balloon.

A crowd formed fast. She got pushed to the back. Cops came, and an ambulance instantly appeared, as if it had been tailing Sonny for blocks, for years. Some guys covered his face, scooped him up and drove off. Cops talked to the driver; he acted pissed, like: I'm already late for work, now this. Got surly, got searched and popped for possession, then thrown into the back of a squad car, screaming. A TV news crew arrived. People fought to be witnesses.

A fireman in boots hosed down the street.

The crowd talked and talked, telling each other what they'd seen.

After a while she walked away.

CHAPTER TEN

I must look lost because I'm always being found. By all kinds of people with plans for me, and all kinds of maps to my future.

Went to church one time with foster parents number three. Didn't work out with them. Long story. Nice people. Anyway, they took me to their church. More nice people; the women in dresses, kids sparkling clean. Minister up front, talking about Sunday stuff. People listening and nodding, little choir singing.

The next thing I know, everybody goes crazy: jabbering and shouting and waving their arms. My foster mom's on the floor; she's laughing and sobbing—

I almost talked in tongues myself, I was so scared.

Lost languages, she told me in the car, going home. A sweet puffy woman. Her name was Winnie. "It's the Holy Spirit moving through you, Lorraine. The Living Ghost."

Dead ghosts were bad enough. I was nine.

"There's only one thing you have to fear, Lorraine. The Devil. He's real."

"I know," I said. My devil didn't have horns, just a stinky yellow T-shirt. My mother's fyon-say, that's what she called him. Throwing kids against the wall. Or foster daddy number two, peeling off his business suit like it was a costume. Locking the door, crawling into my bed. It's okay, he said, we're not related.

Winnie and her husband were really nice. They weren't into sex, even with each other. They couldn't have kids, so they wanted to save me so I could go to heaven and be their little girl.

What will we do there? I'd ask.

Be with God, Winnie said. Adore Him forever. Sometimes heaven sounded like an endless church picnic, people strolling around, eating ice-cream cones and smiling. Other times it sounded like everyone who'd ever died was part of a vast choir, always singing His praises.

I couldn't picture it.

"If I go there and I'm your little girl," I said, "how can you be a little girl with your own mother?"

She'd loved her mom a lot and still missed her. She was always telling me about their happy times together.

"It's kind of hard to understand," she admitted. "But it's all at the same time. It works out fine. And when it's your time to die, God calls you home."

"How does He know my name?"

"Like any father knows his child."

I didn't know mine. There were millions of people in our city alone. How could He keep us all straight?

She thought and thought. "God's God," she said, as if that explained everything.

My family hardly ever talked about God, except when

people died. Then He was everywhere. It's God's will, Granny told me at the funeral home. Home, she called it, as if my brother lived there. My mother screaming and flinging herself on the coffin. Such a tiny little box. How could Bobby breathe in there?

Don't be sad, Granny said later when I couldn't stop crying; God wanted Bobby for his very own. Bobby's with Him in heaven now. And God is always with us.

If He's always with us, why'd He have to take Bobby? Couldn't He drop by the apartment and visit?

It's kind of hard to explain, Granny said. He's in heaven, but He's with us too. He's invisible.

Then how do you know He's here?

You just do.

So you mean He just sat there and watched Bobby die?

My mother slapped me; she thought I was being smart.

I hope there's a heaven and I'll get to see Bobby. But will I be a kid or an old lady? If God's as powerful as everybody says, why doesn't He protect the little children? They didn't do nothing wrong, they didn't hurt anybody.

I've asked lots of people, but no one can tell me.

When someone dies people say, That's too bad, then they hurry away and the world goes on; as if nothing's changed, as if the person didn't matter; as if he were just a dream they'd had and as soon as they woke up, they forgot him.

How can people be alive, then gone so fast? Just gone and you can't see them, you can't touch them or feel them. You keep looking at all the people in the street, like it's all a mistake and any second he'll be there. I thought you were dead. What? You musta been dreaming. Gone, completely gone. You can't believe it. One minute you're walking along together, then suddenly they disappear. They're not beside you anymore. They're not anywhere. A day ago, a minute ago, things were fine and you keep trying to turn back the clock in your mind, but now a door's closed and they're on the other side and you knock and knock but nobody answers.

When people die are they just dead or do their spirits surround us? Do they disappear or go to heaven? I try to believe, but it seems like heaven's something people made up because death's so scary.

I don't want to be alone in the ground somewhere, or sitting on a cloud by myself. I want to BE with someone. I go see Bobby; he's buried in this section for kids. Lost Lambs. My mother bought him a big marble angel, with fancy writing on the stone, Bobby's name and the dates, and the words IN GOD'S HANDS. She never goes there. Granny visits sometimes; last year she planted plastic flowers.

I sit there and talk to him and try not to think about all the bones beneath the grass. Acres of grass, like a big green blanket. I picture Bobby as he was, his cheeks soft and pink, his eyes closed, taking a nap. Just sleeping. I shut my eyes and pretend we're little kids again, crowded into bed or curled up on the floor. But it's not like our house: it's real quiet and peaceful. No yelling or screaming, no cops at the door.

Maybe heaven's like that, a big, quiet room where you sleep beside the people you love. You can't see them or feel them but you can hear them breathing, and there's blankets and everybody's warm.

ChAPTeR ElEVEN

Thank God it's almost Christmas vacation. If I don't get out of here soon I'll be taking hostages in the District Office. Those people are driving me CRAZY. I say we're leaking, and they give me trash cans. I ask for software and get computer paper. If I said I wanted a language lab, they'd send me a foreign exchange student.

It's not just them. I took the car in to be fixed. The guy comes out with this sad look on his face and tells me I should put the car to sleep. I know it's old and tired, will you please just fix it? He says it'll be done the next day. It takes a week. But does he tell me why? Can I get him on the phone?

Sorry, he says when I finally catch him; I've been real busy.

If we're all so busy, why are things so screwed up?

The kids are antsy. They always get like this before Christmas, hoping that for once it will turn out perfect; the whole family hugging. A Hallmark commercial.

Meanwhile, in real life, it's Holiday on Ice Cubes; people drinking and eating WAY too much, fighting tears and each other—

But enough about me.

Brenda's run away again. Nobody's seen her.

Luis came to class wearing gang colors. I sent him home. He hasn't been back.

Janessa's going with a guy too old for me. The other day he picked her up in a brand-new Porsche. I didn't know what it was, of course; the kids told me. I said, That's not her dad, is it? They looked at each other like: Is she for real?

None of this was covered in my Ed. classes.

It was wonderful having Wendy here. We talked and talked then I felt so guilty because the whole time I'm listening to her, I'm thinking: How come SHE gets a husband and children, and students who think she's a fabulous teacher?

I'd file a complaint if I knew where to go. Think how long the line would be.

Last week my doctor asked if I'd considered hormones.

Yes, for my mother! I wanted to shout. What are you saying to me?

Well, she said, when you reach a certain age—

What's certain about it? The other day I burst into tears again, at the supermarket, in the frozen foods section. An old lady said, Are you all right, dear? I said: Everything is so expensive.

I'm just depressed, I told the doctor. Isn't everyone?

No. Had I considered counseling? Or medication?

I've considered everything but a head transplant. I can imagine what she's written on my chart. *Patient is so self-absorbed, she is digesting her brain.*

Mom called last night. Sandy and Rob and the kids will be there Saturday and stay through New Year's. What about me?

Well, I said, I can't stay too long this time.

Why not, Peggy?

Because you'll drive me crazy, asking when I'm going to get married again.

I said: I've made other plans.

Plans? I could practically hear her smiling. Does this involve a man?

Yes! My psychiatrist! I almost shouted.

I said: I've got a lot of work to catch up with over vacation.

Oh, she said. Oh. But that was plenty.

I shouldn't complain. My family loves me. Compared to most of my kids, I've got it made. Scott told me his dad chopped down the Christmas tree. That's nice, I said. In the living room, he added.

There's nothing wrong with my life. I just expected something different. The prince on a white horse. A husband and children.

Wendy asked if I'd considered adoption. Yes, but who'd adopt me? I'm too old, ha-ha. I went to a few meetings for the Fost-Adopt program. Sometimes the children live with you for years while the parents are trying to pull their lives together. If the kids can't be reunited with their families, you can adopt them. But sometimes you have to give the children back. It's okay, the parents say; We're not drug addicts anymore. We promise we won't burn Susie with cigarettes, or let her nearly drown in the bathtub.

I couldn't handle that.

Some people say that all children are wanted. They're talking Gerber babies. We're talking kids with problems: drug babies, AIDS babies, teenagers filled with rage—

Let's face it: I don't have what it takes. By the end of the school day, I'm all used up and it's not enough to save any of them.

I'd better not write my Christmas cards tonight.

Raina came in this morning. Maybe that's why I feel so bleak. I hadn't seen her in weeks. She looked awful.

I said, "You missed the SATs."

She handed me some pages. I was alarmed by what she'd written.

"You sound kind of down," I said. Doy. Suicidal. But I didn't want to put words in her mouth. "Is everything okay?"

She shrugged.

"Where are you staying these days?"

"Around."

"You know you're not supposed to smoke in here."

She ignored me.

"Toby says you're hanging out with some bikers."

"Ain't none of his business what I do."

"Raina, why do you talk like that? Why don't you talk the way you talk on paper?"

She didn't answer.

"It sounds like you're depressed. Have you thought about seeing a counselor?"

"What for?"

"So you can talk about your feelings."

"That'll help."

"It might. Will you be seeing your family over the holidays?"

"Yeah, on *America's Most Wanted.*"

"Do you have any plans for vacation?"

"I'm going skiing at Tahoe. Or maybe to Hawaii. I haven't decided."

"You're welcome to stay at my house, if you'd like. I'll be gone for a few days, but you could make yourself at home." Invite your biker friends over. Hock the furniture for drugs. "When I get back we could spend some time together. Do a little shopping. Rent movies, make popcorn."

"Maybe we could sing some Christmas carols."

"Raina, you're too smart to act like this."

"Like what?"

"You know exactly what I'm talking about. You need to stay on track if you want to go to college."

"College?"

"Have you given any thought to what you'd like to do?"

"Yeah, I'm gonna be a supermodel."

I snapped. I'd had it.

"You don't want me to care? That's fine. That's great. Then quit telling me you're having a hard time."

"Okay." She shoved the pages in her pocket.

"What do you want from me, Raina?"

"Nothing."

"Than why do you keep coming here?"

"It's warm."

"Well, I'm trying to teach. This isn't the Laundromat."

She shrugged. "So teach. Don't let me stop you." She sprawled in her chair, her eyes almost friendly.

"All right, then," I said. "Let's get down to business. The first thing you need to do is put out that cigarette."

She walked to the door, ground it out, and kept going.

I refuse to believe that any child is doomed. But what if her hope is gone?

CHAPTER TWELVE

It seemed like the rain had always been falling, roaring like the traffic outside the Laundromat. She watched through the steamed-up windows, Bert talking. She couldn't hear what he was saying, but it didn't matter; he liked to talk, wouldn't stop if she left.

One morning, she guessed it was Christmas, less traffic, he brought her some clothes and cigarettes. They shared a bottle of his favorite wine and ate Chinese takeout for breakfast.

Then she went to the Plaza and hung around with some friends; she knew their faces not their names, and everybody got real high on downers and drank a lot. She shrieked with laughter.

Drifted in and out of people's apartments. Slept in the Laundromat some nights. Fell down, got up, got loaded, passed out, never sure where she was when she opened her eyes.

For a while she stayed with some Hell's Angels, but they acted too corny, like TV bikers, trashing the place and having stupid fights. The fattest one hit on her all the time, so she told him she had something vague; not AIDS, he would've beaten her up.

Money was tight; Christmas had tapped out the tourists, so she went to the block where the girls hung out, freezing in their miniskirts and short shorts, thighs flashing purple in the neon lights. A few of the girls didn't want her around. One cranky blonde said, I'll keep you in mind the next time someone's looking for a toddler.

But the others were nice, especially the drags, in their sky-high heels and flapping wigs. They treated her kind, like their own child; drove away the pimps and told her who to avoid. It worked out okay except one guy wouldn't pay; he laughed in her face and walked out. And one night she got too stoned and made a big mistake; knew it as soon as he locked the door. She thought: This is it. I'm gonna die. Her mind ran away and hid but came back the next morning and he'd beat her up so bad she had to go to the free clinic.

The doctor scowled when he saw the bruises.

"How old are you?" he asked, examining her face.

"Forty."

"You won't see twenty at this rate."

He stitched her cuts and took X rays and blood. She wanted to leave, but they'd taken her clothes, so she had to wait on the examining table. The paper crinkled when she moved. There was nothing to read and nothing in the cupboards worth taking. The doctor came back with the lab work, sighing.

"You know what I'm going to say, don't you," he said.

She shrugged.

"Why'd you wait so long to come in?"

"I been busy."

He rubbed his face. "We could've done something. Now it's too late."

"I don't want you to do nothing."

"I'll need to examine you and run some tests."

He said a bunch more stuff, but she'd stopped listening. They couldn't make her stay, so she got dressed and left, but once she got outside she didn't know where to go. She could call up Granny but that wouldn't help; all she did was cry and talk about herself, as if she were the star of every show.

She was hungry. No money and she looked like hell. The soup kitchen reeked of all the freaks hunched over bowls. But at least she got to eat, and when they tried to save her soul she pretended she couldn't hear them.

Her toes were frozen. She had to get warm. She could call the teacher, maybe stay in her house, but she'd probably steal something, then school would be over and there'd be nothing. There had to be something.

She bummed some change—the bruises helped—and took the bus to the roller rink. It was warm and dark inside. No one stared at her face and the place was so loud, she didn't have to think; the roaring skates and blades filled up her head, and the music played and the lights were twinkling.

She watched families swoop by, children with their parents and groups of teenagers playing crack the whip. The deejay said, "Couples only this time," and a parade of old people circled the rink, turning this way and that like square dancers. Young couples glided by, holding hands. She and Sonny had pretended they were in the

Olympics, his arm around her waist. They never lost their balance, even when the strobe lights made their faces dance. He was always so graceful until things went bad and he lost track of what to do with his arms and legs.

She put on her skates and entered the rink, moving slowly at first, then picking up speed, cutting through the skaters like a Roller Derby queen. Big, nasty gals on wheels. Don't mess with me. Her mother used to watch them on TV. Saturday afternoons, beer cans and babies on the floor. Where's Bobby? Dammit, Raina, I told you to watch him. He's getting in my purse again. . . . The packs circling the rink, then clashing on the rail in a snarl of flashing fists and yellow hair.

She paused to catch her breath. A boy skated up beside her.

"Hi." He smiled. He had a baby face and glasses. "I've been watching you. You skate real good."

"Thanks."

"You come here often?"

"No."

She took off. The deejay said, "Let's turn back the clock," and played a song she'd never heard.

He was beside her again, his braces gleaming. "I come here a lot. What grade are you in?"

She pulled ahead. He stumped along behind her.

"I'm seventeen," he called. "How old are you?"

She was too small, that was the problem. People thought she was a puppy they could pick up and put in their pockets. All she wanted to do was think about Sonny, and this stupid kid was ruining it.

"You got a boyfriend?"

She lost him, streaking through the skaters until the breeze was blowing on the sparkling bay and the sun was shining. She and Sonny were sailing. He looked so strong. He knew exactly what to do. He used to have a boat, and a mother, and a life. Let's not think about that now, Sonny said; let's be happy.

But the kid was in her face, the lights bouncing off his glasses.

"Why are you acting so stuck-up?" he said.

"Leave me alone, okay?"

"I'm just being friendly."

She stopped skating and faced him. "Listen to me, you stupid little twit. Go find somebody else to play with."

He looked so shocked, she almost laughed. Then he was staring at a knife like he couldn't figure out how it got in his hand. "You shouldn't act so rude," he said. The knife swung out and ripped her jacket.

She jumped back and flew, but she couldn't lose him. Round and round the rink, the music blaring, the strobe lights flashing in some weird dream where he was trying to kill her and nobody noticed. She glanced over her shoulder. His face was blank.

She sailed out of the rink to the snack bar, the street, down the sidewalk, dodging traffic, through the crosswalk, people shouting, the kid calmly knocking down an old man in his way.

Saw a cop car ahead. Didn't stop; she'd be dead. Burst into a store past a rent-a-cop running, walkie-talkie squawking, down aisles crammed with clothes, to the housewares section; startled faces, glass smashing, the kid behind her crashing through shoppers and displays.

Out a door to the street, down some steps, almost fell. Legs shuddering, heart thumping, her breath the only sound now in the world.

There was nowhere to go.

Maybe Bert would help her. The Laundromat was empty. She ricocheted off a washer toward the bathroom door. Was it locked? Jesus God. Fingers fumbling with the knob. Wrenched it open, pulled it shut, turned the bolt.

The kid slammed into the door. He pleaded and howled, he kicked and snarled, fists raining on the wood. She crouched beneath the sink. The kid finally calmed down. He kneeled on the floor and put his mouth beneath the door and said, "Why'd you have to do that? That was rude."

It got real quiet, but she didn't move. She couldn't understand what had made her keep running. Why was she trying so hard to stay alive? Why hadn't she run toward the knife, like Sonny?

A long while later Bert came back.

CHAPTER THIRTEEN

It seems amazing that anyone can have a baby, like a puppy in a box outside Safeway. You want one? You got one. You don't need any training. You can even be on drugs or drunk or crazy.

I see these little girls with their big bellies. They think they're growing somebody to love them, someone who'll never go away. They're happy because people are finally paying attention; asking, How're you feeling? When's the baby due? They're important; they've got appointments to go to, and doctors and nurses who care what they do.

Then it hurts like hell and the party's over and the baby's screaming and they're all alone.

I see them bouncing their crying babies. I say: Just hold them still and close. But the girls don't listen or look at the babies; they're watching the door to see who's coming in. Maybe it's the dealer or their speedfreak boyfriend, still looking cute, he hasn't lost his teeth.

The girls want to play. I'll be right back, they say, handing the baby to whoever's around. Here's his bottle, he likes Pepsi. Then they're out the door. For an hour or a day, sometimes longer.

The girls don't nurse their babies. They think it makes them look ignorant.

Sometimes I hold the babies and I feel so bad. I look into their innocent eyes and think: You could've been born to anyone, but you had the bad luck to get stuck with a kid who doesn't know enough to support your head and forgets to change your diaper till it's dripping.

You can call the county and make a report, but nothing happens unless the kid's practically dead.

When I was little lots of people came to our house: teachers and social workers and cops. The cops scared my mother, but she told the others: It's none of your business WHAT I do. She'd made us; she could do whatever she wanted. One social worker told my mother not to hit me. Like this? Looking right at the woman while she did it. The woman left. They all did; there were so few of them and so many of us. In the places where we lived, all the families were like ours: apartments crawling with lice and mice and kids. One social worker went out on the balcony to smoke. I said, You better not stand there; sometimes people get shot.

People think kids get used to where they live, but we were scared every single minute.

I hid inside books. And I liked going to school. There were bells and snacks and assignments and rules. But homework was hard; you could never find a pencil, or a clean place to put the papers down. And it was always so noisy: the TV blaring those scary movies my mother loved; chainsaw massacres and vampire zombies, the little kids watching, their eyes bugging out.

You need a home to do homework. So sometimes I didn't do it. My teachers thought I was making up excuses.

I've seen your house, stood outside in the dark. So many rooms with nobody in them. We never had enough beds. Or socks or toothbrushes. We never brushed our teeth. No one taught us what to do. Ray was a boy, he didn't have to do nothing, so Sheila got stuck taking care of us but after a while she got sick of watching kids and ran off with this guy and got married and pregnant. He beat her up bad and she begged to come home but my mother said No, you made your bed. Sheila standing in the hall, tears running down her face. Please let her stay, Mom, I said, but she wouldn't.

After Sheila left, things got wild. My mother was gone a lot. She'd come home flying. People were spying on her, she said, watching her from the rooftops with binoculars. I'd see my brothers in the street; they'd wave and keep going like I was part of something they'd left behind. Sometimes I missed school because I had to watch Bobby, but I didn't mind. He loved me best. He'd sit on my lap and we'd look at books. He was such a smart baby. He learned so fast.

One time it got late and my mother didn't come home and there wasn't any heat and Bobby was freezing, so I wrapped him in a blanket. There was nothing to eat so I asked the neighbors and they gave us some wieners and milk. When my mother came back and found out she was pissed, like I'd done it just to make her look bad.

After Bobby died lots of people came around, asking questions and investigating. They went away again and nothing changed but me. Then my mother had Brandy, but I never really knew her; I was doing the foster care thing.

You read about these girls in the newspaper who don't know they're pregnant until the baby drops out. People say, she must've known. But sometimes the girl doesn't. She doesn't want to know. She's completely freaking out. So she keeps getting loaded so she won't have to think, so she doesn't have to notice her swollen belly. Trying to get so loaded, she passes out. Hopes she never wakes up, because she feels so guilty.

What if the baby's screwed up and it's all her fault?

Miss Johnson, I'm so scared. Please help me.

ChaPTeR FOURTeeN

I almost burst into tears when I read what she'd written.

"Are you telling me you're pregnant?"

She started to reach for a cigarette, then put the pack away.

"How far along are you?"

She shrugged. "A ways."

"Have you been to the doctor?"

"Yeah."

"What did they say?"

"Don't know," she said. "I didn't listen."

My fingers itched to slap her, hard. Someone had beat me to it.

"What happened to your face?"

"Nothing."

"What is it, some kind of teenage thing? You break out in bruises?"

"It's a long story."

"Your mother do that?"

She smiled.

"Your boyfriend?"

"No. Forget it."

I was trembling, I was so upset.

"You come into my classroom, tell me you're pregnant, looking like you were dragged down the street on your face—"

"It was just some guy."

"Did you call the police?"

"They wouldna cared."

"Why not?"

"It was a trick."

"What kind of trick?" Duhhh.

"You know. A john."

I felt as if the top of my head had lifted off and was shooting around the room.

"You're selling your body?"

"I ran out of Girl Scout cookies."

"This isn't a joke!" Tears filled my throat. "What about the baby? What about AIDS?"

"I'm careful."

"Careful!"

"There's ways," she said. "Anyway, the baby's father used. But he hardly ever shared needles."

I've heard so many sad stories in this room, so many tearful variations on this theme. I'm pregnant, Miss Johnson. What should I do?

"Have you had an AIDS test?"

"No."

"Why not?"

"I'm scared." Fear wiped away the sneer. She looked like what she was: a child.

"Raina, you've got to think about this. You've got to

make some important decisions."

"I know. I was thinking maybe you could help me."

It's too late! I wanted to shout. I wanted to run out of the room. I wanted to lay my head down on the desk and sob.

"Have you talked to your family?"

"Yeah. My mother."

"What did she say?"

"Too bad."

"That's it?"

"She said to call back. She was doing something."

"What about the baby's father?"

"He's dead. He got in an accident."

"I'm sorry."

Her eyes filled with tears. "We were gonna be married. He would've been a real good daddy."

Oh yes, junkies make wonderful parents.

I had never felt so angry.

"Well," I said finally, "let's consider your options." Let's write them on the blackboard in chalk. Let's review the alternatives. Discuss the pros and cons. "Have you thought about having an abortion?"

"No."

"Why not?"

"It's wrong."

"But it's not wrong to smoke and drink and take drugs while you're pregnant."

She wouldn't look at me. "It's too late," she said.

She lifted her ripped coat. Beneath the layers of dirty clothes was a mound of hard white belly.

I thought I was going to vomit through my nose. I thought I was going to choke her. A humming in my head got louder, closer. But I am a professional.

"What about letting the baby be adopted?"

"Maybe." She slumped in her chair. "I don't know."

"You can't take care of a baby. You know that."

"I could go on welfare and get an apartment."

"Raina, you can't be serious."

"I'm old enough."

"To be someone's mother?"

"I took care of my brother." Tears filmed her eyes.

"What happened to Bobby? Raina, please tell me."

"It wasn't my fault!"

"Of course it wasn't. You were too young to be responsible for Bobby. You're still too young. You need time to grow up."

"It's too late now."

"No, it isn't, Raina. There are lots of people who would love this baby and give it a wonderful home."

"Not if it's all screwed up. And people will know I'm the one who did it."

She cradled her head in her arms and sobbed. I should've kept my mouth shut. But I didn't.

"It's a little late to think about that now, isn't it? Where was your head, Raina? You're not some idiot. Have you ever heard of fetal alcohol syndrome? There are people who would die to have a baby. They try and try but nothing happens. While people like you keep pumping them out, and the kids have kids and it goes on and on. Look at your family. The damage. My God. What's the matter with people? Can't they see what's going on? We're producing a nation of pinheads!"

I paused to wipe the froth from my lips and noticed someone standing in the doorway.

"Superintendent Kelley," I said, "so nice of you to drop in."

CHAPTER FIFTEEN

The teacher was rich; why did she drive a piece of shit? Raina could not believe the car when she got in. The upholstery was shot. The windshield was cracked. They were up to their knees in empty Cheetos bags.

Miss Johnson looked embarrassed.

She waved to the Superintendent, who drove by looking grim. She said, "It's fun to make new friends, isn't it," and pulled into the traffic.

They got stuck on a hill when the gearshift locked. Cars piled up behind them, horns blaring.

"My God," the teacher moaned, "this is a nightmare."

"Why don't you get a new car?" It was the first thing she'd said since she'd gotten in.

"Good idea. Let's leave this one here." The teacher wrestled the car into first, and they lurched across the intersection.

The teacher's house was warm. Some lights were already on.

"Let me take your coat. How did this get ripped?"

"A guy tried to stab me."

"You're kidding."

"No."

The teacher's mouth opened and closed. Then she said, "Can I get you a soda?"

The kitchen smelled clean. The fridge was full of stuff. The teacher eyed a bottle of wine.

"Go ahead," Raina said. She didn't miss much. "It's too late to be a bad influence."

The teacher looked startled. "That's okay. I'm just thirsty."

She opened a bottle of mineral water. Raina chose cranberry juice.

"Sit down, make yourself at home. I'll get supper going. Are you hungry?"

"Yeah." Her stomach rumbled, and the baby kicked. It had been moving for months, but she'd refused to notice. The baby had been a secret she wouldn't even tell herself.

She sat on the couch in the living room. There were pictures on the walls and shelves of books. She longed to stretch out and close her eyes, but the teacher was saying something.

". . . not much of a cook. I usually have a sandwich and soup. Or pasta and salad. Would you rather have that?"

"Whatever."

The only time she'd been in a house like this was when she and Sonny had broken in. His dad had changed the locks, so they smashed a window, but most of the stuff they took was Sonny's, so it wasn't really stealing.

What would it be like to live in a house with clean

soft carpets and shaded lamps and towels in the bathroom and baskets of plants and magazines fanned across
the coffee table?

"I'm defrosting some chicken," the teacher
announced, setting down a plate of cheese and crackers.
"Is that okay? Are you a vegetarian?"

"I'll eat ants."

The teacher smiled as if she had gas and sat in a chair
across from the couch.

"So," she said. "Pretty cold tonight."

"Yeah."

"Are you warm enough? Shall I turn up the heat?"

"I'm fine."

"Are you sure? Shall I make a fire?"

"You don't have to."

"I'd be glad to."

The teacher jumped up and started crumpling news-
papers. She fed the fire, and it leaped to life. It felt odd to
be in the teacher's house; as odd as it felt to have someone
in her belly.

For a long time they watched the flames dance.

Then the teacher apologized again. She said she
never should have gone off like that and made those
remarks about Raina's family; her behavior had been
completely unprofessional. It wasn't Raina's fault she
couldn't have a baby. And wasn't it incredible, I mean
talk about ironic, that the Superintendent chose that
moment to show up?

"Life's funny," she added unconvincingly.

"Yeah."

"I really am sorry, Raina."

"That's okay."

Her mother never apologized for anything, as if it would make her seem small and weak and she had to stay big and tough. She wouldn't say sorry no matter what. Not even for Bobby.

"I better go check the chicken."

Raina took off her shoes and slid onto the rug, as close to the fire as she could get. She knew what the teacher was thinking: Now what?

She's afraid she's stuck with me, Raina thought, like a lost dog nobody wants. Anyway, it wasn't like she could stay there forever and the baby and the problems would disappear. That wasn't going to happen. What was going to happen?

The teacher was shaking her gently, saying, "Do you still want to eat? Then you can hit the hay."

"Okay." She was instantly awake. It was always safer that way.

They sat at either end of a long table. Raina ate while the teacher tried to make conversation.

"It seems funny to be here together, doesn't it. I mean, instead of at school."

"Yeah."

"We'll figure out what to do tomorrow. Tonight you can get a good rest."

"Okay."

"Thank God it's Friday."

"It is?"

"What a week. Do you ever have a week like— it's just been crazy."

There was chocolate chip ice cream for dessert.

"Can I get you something else? Would you like some tea?"

Raina didn't want tea but she said yes because it felt so good to be waited on. They drank their tea and watched the fire die then the teacher showed her to the guest room.

Imagine having a room for people who didn't even live there. She had never had a room to herself. There was a quilt on the bed and pretty things on the bureau. Raina picked up a tiny glass doll and saw the teacher's eyes reflected in the mirror.

"Don't worry," she said, "I won't take nothing."

"Of course you won't." The teacher looked ashamed.

She gave Raina a nightgown and a toothbrush and a towel for her very own bathroom, right next door. There were blankets in the closet, if she needed more. Then she said she'd see her in the morning.

Raina washed up and pulled on the nightgown. It was way too big and smelled clean and fresh. The pillowcase was embroidered with flowers. The blankets felt heavy on her legs.

I shoulda took a shower, she thought, then her eyes closed and she slept.

When she woke up the next morning the teacher was gone. She'd left a note on the kitchen table: *I'll be back soon. Make yourself at home.*

Raina wandered through the house looking into all the rooms. It felt strange having so much space to herself. Strange but good. She had toast and juice, then stayed in the shower forever. The baby kicked. She watched her belly ripple, the tiny wave rolling beneath the skin; wondering: Who's in there?, the thought so scary, she let it drift away and just washed her hair. Then she dried herself and put her clothes back on.

The teacher returned with bread from the bakery and a big bag of clothes from Penney's. She said, "I hope these fit. I guessed at the sizes. You're so little it kind of makes it tough."

"Yeah, it's hard to find maternity stuff in the kid's section. Thanks," Raina said. "You didn't need to."

The bag was full of underwear and pajamas and sweatshirts and three pairs of jeans with stretchy panels in front. When she pulled on the pants, her stomach popped out like a sigh she'd been holding in for months.

For lunch they had cold chicken and salad and bread. The teacher had bought her a big jug of milk. How long is that supposed to last? she wondered. How long am I going to be here?

Then it was time to talk. She didn't want to. She wanted to smoke a cigarette, but the teacher would have a fit. Besides, she couldn't do that anymore; there was the baby to consider.

She hadn't meant to have a baby, wasn't trying to get pregnant. When the pills ran out she forgot to get more. At the time it hadn't seemed important; Sonny usually couldn't make love.

"Let's sit in the living room," the teacher said.

She sat on the couch while the teacher built a fire. Rain blew against the windows. She felt so odd, sitting in this house in her stiff new clothes, as if she were wearing someone else's body.

She wanted to get things over with; to say or do something so crazy and stupid, the teacher would throw her out. She wanted to live in this house forever. She wanted to crawl inside the teacher's heart.

The teacher said, "I'm in kind of a delicate position here, Raina. I'm not supposed to interfere in your private life."

"I don't mind."

"It's the sort of thing Superintendent Kelley wouldn't like. I seem to remember him mentioning that."

"Me too."

"Now here you are, sitting in my house. I could get in a lot of trouble."

"Join the club."

"Do you understand what I'm saying?"

"Yeah. But it's not his choice. Or yours. It's mine."

"Exactly." The teacher nodded, smiling. "Now we're on the same page."

"That's a weird saying. We're not on a page; we're in real life."

"It's just an expression. The thing is, Raina, you've got to figure out what to do."

"How?"

"What do you want to do?"

"I don't know."

"It appears that it's too late for an abortion. Would you say that's correct?"

"Yeah."

"That leaves you two options: Try to raise the baby yourself, or give it up for adoption."

"I don't want to give my baby away."

"We're not talking about leaving it in a box outside Safeway. We're talking about finding a family for the baby. A real home. There's nothing wrong with that, Raina. Sometimes that's the most loving thing a mother can do."

"I know." Of course she couldn't keep the baby. What

kind of life could she give it when she didn't have a life herself? But she knew how it felt to be unwanted, rejected. How could she do that to her own child?

"You're right," she said, "but I feel so bad."

"It's one of those times when none of the choices are good ones. I'm sorry, honey."

The word made her want to cry. She said, "What if you kept it?"

"Me?" The teacher looked alarmed.

"You said you always wanted a baby."

"Yes, but that was a long time ago. I'm too old now."

"How old?"

"Forty-five."

"That's pretty old."

"I wouldn't say that. It's just that—things are different now."

"You can have it, if you want. I trust you."

The teacher shook her head. "I can't take your baby."

"You'd be the mother. I'd just visit sometimes."

"It's not that simple. Raina, listen to me, please. I'm glad you trust me, I really am. But I can't keep your baby. I promise you we'll find a wonderful family who'll love this baby as their very own and give it a wonderful life. The kind of life you should've had. You can still be happy. But you've got to think this through, Raina."

"You're not just saying that 'cause you think it's fucked up and you don't want a fucked-up kid?"

The teacher frowned. "Of course not. Babies are very resilient."

"I might've drunk too much. I did crank sometimes." She could kill herself from shame and guilt, but the baby would die too.

"We have to assume that the baby's fine and take it from there. That's all we can do. You need to take care of yourself, Raina. Eat the right foods, go to the doctor. And not smoke or drink or take any drugs."

"I'm not." It was probably too late. "I stopped."

"You're welcome to stay here until the baby's born. We can call some adoption agencies next week. We'll figure everything out. If that's what you really want."

Her heart soared, but her voice was flat. "It probably wouldn't work, me staying here."

"Why not?"

She struggled to put her thoughts into words. "There's inside cats and outside cats. I'm kind of an outside cat."

The teacher smiled. "Actually, you're not a cat at all."

"It's just an expression. You might not like me around."

"I like you fine."

"You could get in trouble."

The teacher shrugged. "What else is new?"

"You're sure?"

"I'm sure."

"Okay, then," Raina said.

It was settled, like that. She wasn't alone; the teacher was going to help her. She felt as if she'd stepped outside herself and into a new life.

Later, the teacher had to meet a friend.

"We're going to the movies. I'll be home before supper. I'll bring back some ice cream, to celebrate."

"Celebrate what?"

"Our collaboration. Do you have a favorite?"

"Chocolate's fine."

The teacher put on her coat and left. How does she know I won't steal stuff? Raina wondered. How does she know I won't wreck everything?

She curled up on the couch with a magazine and read for a while, then fell asleep. When she opened her eyes she didn't know where she was. Then she remembered. She felt happy.

She went into the kitchen for a glass of milk and filled a pretty plate with crackers and cheese. Then she noticed the phone, the goddamn phone. Her mother had said to call her back. Not that she cared what Raina did. But maybe she'd be different because of the baby. Maybe just this once—don't be a chump.

If only the teacher were there.

"Hey, Ma."

"Where were you? You were supposed to call."

"I did. We're on the phone right now." She heard her mother light a cigarette, almost felt the comfort of the smoke in her lungs.

"So how's it feel to be having a baby?"

"Okay, I guess."

"I got it all figured out. You can get on welfare and get an apartment with Lyn and the baby. That asshole Gary kicked her out."

"I don't need an apartment."

"How come?"

"I'm staying with this teacher."

"What teacher?"

"From school. I'm giving up the baby, Ma. I can't keep it."

Her mother's silence was worse than words.

"I don't got any choice. I'm too young to be a mother."

"You'd give away your baby, your flesh and blood? What kind of person are you?"

"Ma, listen. I can't have a baby." But her thoughts wouldn't come out in the teacher's words. "I got nowhere to stay."

"Weren't you listening to me? You can get on welfare and get a place. Lyn and the baby can move right in. They been staying here. She's driving me crazy."

"But Ma, I can't take care of a baby. I don't know how."

"Don't worry, I'll help you."

"I'm too messed up. The teacher says—"

"Who you gonna listen to, your mother or some stranger? She probably wants to steal the baby for herself."

"No, she don't want it."

"People always want something."

"She's gonna help me find a good family for the baby." She shouldna said that. Her mother blew up.

"What's wrong with the one you got? Jesus Christ, Raina, I don't believe you! How would you like it if I'd gave you away?"

"You did. Remember all those foster homes?"

"Because you were acting like a little slut!"

"That's not true! You never listened to me!"

"Do we have to go into all that now? We're talking about your kid. My grandchild."

No, let's talk about me, Raina thought. I wanted you to hug me, but you pushed me away like a puppy crawling back on its belly; begging: Please don't hurt me. Please, just love me.

"You're not thinking about an abortion, are you?"

"No," Raina said. "It's too late."

"I told Lyn if she did, she was out of the family. Now she's glad. The baby's so cute. He doesn't look a bit like Gary."

"Ma, I don't know." She could feel herself sinking, like her mother was some big wave crashing down. Then lifting her up.

Maybe things would be different.

"You better come home."

"Right now? It's raining."

"So take the bus."

"I can't. I'm broke."

"Get your teacher friend to give you some money."

"She's gone. Maybe I should wait till she gets home."

She could hear her mother breathing, her lighter snapping shut. Then she quietly said, "You're scared, aren't you?"

"No. About what?"

"The baby," her mother said. "You and me."

"Not really."

"Things have changed. I wanna talk to you, Raina."

Her heart was pounding. "Do you think maybe you could come and get me?"

"I'd love to, baby, but the car's not running. We'll talk when you get home, okay?"

She found money for the bus in a jar on the counter, taking only what she needed, not another dime. She made her bed and got the bag of clothes, then sat down in the kitchen with a pen and some paper.

She tried to write a note that explained everything, so the teacher would understand, and would know how much she appreciated stuff. But the paper she left on the table was blank.

Chapter Sixteen

She woke with him in her head every morning, like still being drunk after a bad night; not the way he was just before he died but the way he'd been when they'd met and she'd thought: Everything will be all right now.

Her mother banged dirty dishes in the sink until Raina opened her eyes.

"You were supposed to do these."

"It's Lyn's turn."

Lyn and Brandy and the baby were still asleep. Her mother shared the other bedroom with Don, who didn't have a clue he was on his way out. He'd told Raina he was going to be her new daddy, while her mother made faces behind his back.

Raina stretched on the couch. Her shoulders ached. "Can't you make this thing more comfortable?"

"Yeah, put a board over it."

Her mother was pissed. It was cold, it was early, and she had to go to work while everyone else could stay in bed, then sit around all day, watching television. Lyn loved the home shopping shows. "I'm gonna get me one of those," she'd say, pointing a potato chip at the set. Last night her mother told her she was getting too fat. "Well, look at you!" Lyn said, and they really got into it, while Raina wished she was anywhere else and Don drank beer and watched *Bonanza*.

She climbed off the couch and went into the bathroom. There was a mirror on the door, streaked with toothpaste and soap. She undressed and examined the shelf of her belly. How had she allowed this baby to happen? Why had she ever come home? Or thought for one second—

Her mother pounded on the door. "I gotta get in there! It's my house, remember?"

The door was locked. She turned on the shower.

"You better be out by the time I'm dressed!"

HELLO, I'M CARLA! HOW CAN YOU HELP ME? What did her mother expect her to do? She'd been to the county, she'd filled out the papers; she'd get her own place when the money came through. She was sick of picking up after her sisters and Don, and everyone else who kept blowing in; her brothers and Sheila, their packs of kids, her mother's girlfriends who crashed on the couch because they were too screwed up to drive home.

When that happened, Raina slept on the floor. Oh, she don't mind, her mother would tell them.

She came out of the bathroom and started coffee. When it was done she handed her mother a cup.

"You better call the county again," her mother said.

"I did. They said it'll take about a week."

"And tell your lazy sister to get off her butt and clean

up that room today. It looks like a pigpen."

No matter what her mother said, she loved Lyn best. She brought things home for Lyn and the baby and paid for Jimmy's picture to be taken at the store. There were big framed pictures of Jimmy on the wall, and pictures of Brandy and Sheila and Willie. Pictures of everyone but Bobby and her.

"And don't forget to go to the Laundromat." Her mother lit a smoke and was out the door.

Raina did the dishes. The baby was kicking. Then she sponged the counters and scrubbed the floor so she wouldn't have to think. She wasn't writing anymore. She didn't want to see her thoughts on paper; didn't want to picture the teacher's face and how it must've looked when she came home that night and realized Raina was gone.

She hadn't been back to school. What was the point? Anyway, the teacher must hate her. She wanted to smoke and drink, go crazy, and no one would care; they wouldn't say nothing, but she couldn't do that to the baby.

Don came out of the bedroom and helped himself to coffee. He was like a million of her mother's boyfriends, always talking about how things were gonna change any-day; he was gonna drive a truck for twenty bucks an hour, then he'd buy a new car, and on and on. He was mean to the kids when her mother was gone; hauled them onto his lap when she was there.

He lit a cigarette. "You going to the store?"

"You got any money?"

"Your mother give you some?"

"For the Laundromat. She said to give me a ride."

"The battery's dead."

He never wanted to help; he said it hurt his back. Lyn wouldn't help, but Brandy might. She liked her little sister. They'd talked last night. She'd told her she should be going to school, not running drugs for the dealer down the hall. I know, I know, Brandy had sighed. Ten years old and she looked worn out.

"Man," Don said. "The weather's sure ugly."

The day was gray. Rain pounded on the street. Her jacket wouldn't zip up over her stomach. She'd have to take the bus to her appointment, then do the wash and get dinner going. Her mother liked to eat as soon as she got home.

Why was she the one who did everything, while Lyn sat around and played with Jimmy, and Don filled the air with his bullshit and smoke? She was sick of people trying to make her do stuff; the teacher, her mother, the girl at the county, her fingernails so long and pointy, she'd bleed to death if she picked her nose. She'd told Raina that after the baby was born she had to go to school to get welfare money.

"Kinda like blackmail."

The girl's eyes got cold. "We think of it as an incentive."

Raina went into the bathroom and locked the door. If she didn't lock it, Don might barge in. Oops, he'd say, I didn't know you was in there. Lyn just laughed, but it made her sick.

She took the bus and got off at the Clinic. It was crowded with women and restless kids. A girl with a big belly sat beside her. When she got called, another girl came in and took the girl's place and her magazine and smiled until she caught Raina's eye.

"When you due?"

"Don't know," Raina said. "Pretty soon."

"Me too. If it's a boy I'm naming him Torrance. It's T-o-r-e-n-t-s, I guess. I heard it on my soap opera."

"Oh."

"If it's a girl I'm naming her Brooklyn."

"Brooklyn?"

"Or Dawn or Sundance, I can't decide."

The girl's face was a cross between pretty and odd, as if she'd been bred in a womb full of soda pop. Raina looked around the room. If faces could be bought, everyone's would've come from Kmart. Hers too.

"Whaddya going to name your baby?"

"I don't know."

"A name's real important. Think about it. It makes people see you a certain way."

These girls gave their babies fancy names that ended up sounding like cigarette brands. Raina thought: You can name your baby anything you want, but the world's gonna call it Hey You.

The girl's name was called. She said, "I hope it's not the doctor with ice-cold hands. Good luck."

"You too."

Raina waited and waited, the baby kicking at the small of her back. A nurse finally took her down a long hall, weighed her, then put her in a tiny room. She undressed and waited on the examining table. Dr. Ramirez bustled in and washed her hands.

"How are you feeling today, Raina?"

"Okay."

"Any changes since the last time? Have you noticed any contractions?"

"Yeah, the little cramps. Does that mean the baby's coming?"

"No, not yet. Did you check into that childbirth class?"

"I'm gonna."

"You don't have a lot of time." The doctor spoke calmly, but Raina had seen that look all her life. She wanted to say: You couldn't possibly despise me as much as I despise myself.

"Lie down, please."

Raina stared at the ceiling. Someone had taped up a picture of a tiger and her cubs.

"You're one centimeter dilated."

"What's that mean?"

"It means you better take that class." The doctor spread cold jelly on Raina's belly and they listened to the heartbeat, strong and fast. "Okay, you can sit up."

Raina drew the gown around her.

"You remember what we talked about the last time."

"Yeah."

"So you're not smoking or drinking. Or doing any drugs."

She almost said: What kind of person do you think I am? But she didn't want to hear the answer.

"No."

The doctor scribbled on a pad. "Take this to the lab. I want you to get an AIDS test."

"Why?" Her heart almost froze. "Do you think there's something wrong with the baby?"

"No. But under the circumstances, we have to make

sure. Did you ever have unprotected sex?"

"Well, yeah, obviously."

"I mean more than once."

She hadn't meant to, but she couldn't be sure. Sometimes she'd been so drunk.

"I don't think so."

The doctor looked like she wanted to say something but just handed her the piece of paper.

She put her clothes back on and made her next appointment, then headed down the hall to the lab. The technician tied her off and took a sample of her blood and gave her a number to call for the results.

"But give it a couple of weeks," he said. "At the moment we're kind of backed up."

In the meantime how was she supposed to eat or sleep? If the baby was sick it was all her fault. And Sonny's too, but he was gone.

She was so scared. She wanted to talk to someone, but Granny would cry and change the subject and Lyn only heard what was on the TV. Her mother would say: What'd you expect? Lie down with dogs, get up with fleas. Anyway, you don't got AIDS; you're just skinny. Too bad that's not contagious, huh, Lyn?

She wished she could talk to the teacher.

She could picture the teacher's worried face, hear her soft voice saying, Raina, what about you? You might be sick too.

That didn't matter. If she was sick, she'd die and everything would stop. Then she'd just be dead or maybe there'd be heaven, and if heaven was real, she could be with Bobby. Unless God sent her straight to hell.

ChAPTER SEVENTEEN

She was trying as hard as she could to relax, to empty her mind of desire and thought, but sitting cross-legged on the floor hurt her knees, and the rug really needed to be vacuumed.

The book advised: *Let your thoughts flow through you like a river running toward the sea.* But she could see the pile of papers on the dining room table, waiting to be read and graded. She closed her eyes. The phone rang. The machine picked up the call.

"Peggy, are you there?" Her mother's voice, laced with a trace of impatience and hurt. She took the phone machine personally, as if it had been bought for the purpose of screening out her calls. "Are you home, Peg? I just wanted to say hi." I'm not getting up. I'll call her tomorrow. But what if she dies tonight? We found her by the phone, Peg. Clutching the receiver. The doctor says you broke her heart.

She reached for the phone as her mother hung up.

Relax. Breathe deeply. Let thoughts flow through you

like a river running toward the sea. She'd been a Girl Scout the last time she'd sat like this easily, but if she lay down to meditate, she'd fall asleep; woke up the other night drooling into the rug. Which needed to be vacuumed, very badly.

Relax. Breathe deeply. Focus only on the moment and the air flowing into and out of your nose. Jeff had come to class stoned, reeking of dope. His eyes were so red, they glowed. No, man, he'd insisted; it's allergies. Then what's that smell? Don't know, he'd said; it must be my aftershave lotion.

What was wrong with her? She was trying to stay focused, but sitting like this made her butt hurt. Forget about your butt. There's nothing wrong with your butt. That losing thirty pounds wouldn't cure. See what you're doing? That negative thinking? You're not managing your stress; it's managing you. What she really needed was a twelve-step group for people addicted to self-help books. She could retire on what she'd already spent.

Empty your mind of confusion and doubt. Embrace your thoughts, then let them go. There is only this moment. And all those papers on the table. All those misspelled words, incomplete sentences, double negatives. She don't know nothing. She hadn't heard from Raina. The kids said she was back with her mom.

How on earth could Raina have been so stupid? If she didn't stay in school she was doomed. Can't she see she's repeating the pattern: alcohol and drugs, and babies too soon, so the whole damn thing goes on and on?

It made her want to scream.

But I feel so calm. Serenity is spreading through my body. There's nothing I can do. She doesn't want my help. Sometimes childhood is such a deep wound, the resulting adult is merely scar tissue. Gee, that's deep. You can't write her off like that. She's just a kid. Her eyes look dead. But there's a baby growing in her belly.

Why wasn't it ever my turn? It isn't fair! All those visits to the doctor, all those stupid tests. Thinking: This is it! Then the spots of blood. Oh, dear God, no. Don't let this happen . . . I don't want her baby. It's probably messed up. Now you're writing off a helpless infant! You used to think love answered every question. But life's too big, and I'm too small. Except for my butt. What time is it? I should call Mom back, but she'll say, Where were you? and I'll say, On the floor, and she'll say, Doing what? Meditating, I'll say. Then she'll say—why call her? I can have the conversation by myself.

A mantra might help. I feel so peaceful. These jeans are so tight I can barely breathe. Teacher found dead. Foul play ruled out. Official cause of death: her pants.

Will you knock it off? No one cares about your body. Boo hoo, poor me. Don't even start. I should go to the gym, take a yoga class. A frozen yogurt class. Will you give yourself a break? It's not like you have to wear a WIDE LOAD sign. You bought that stupid membership, you might as well use it. Exercise more. That's good for stress. You don't need to starve, just cut back on the junk food. I wonder if Raina is eating.

Forget about Raina. Forget about her baby. You are deeply relaxed, so completely at peace that there is only this moment. And all that ice cream in the freezer. You shouldn't buy that stuff. Shouldn't keep it in the house. Just bring a spoon and eat it in the store.

Enough. Empty your mind. Let thoughts flow through

you like a river running toward the sea. But how could she go back to her mother? She jumps into the flames, trying to warm herself, and freezes to death, again and again.

Does anybody really care? Does the Superintendent think school is important for these kids, or does he view it as a holding tank, jail with grades? At least while they're in class they're not stealing his hubcaps. Doesn't he realize—I am so wise. It's a wonder the world isn't breaking down my door. Margaret Johnson: Sees all, knows all. Ask me anything. And pass the Cheetos.

Shut up and be serene. Let thoughts flow through you like a nose running to the sea. Ricky's out sick. Or so the story goes. It doesn't do any good to call his parents. Half the time no one answers and when they do, it's like, Ricky who? Oh, yeah, our son. He went to school. No, he didn't. Are you sure? Positive; his chair is empty. Well, I don't know, he's around here someplace. . . .

If I'd had a child—but you didn't. You didn't. The problem is, you can't accept it. You're either looking back, or ahead, with dread, so you're never in the present. It escapes your attention.

Which may have something to do with my inability to focus. On my nose or anything else.

It's time to move ahead, to get on with my life, not keep waiting for everything to fall into place. Mr. Right gallops up on his white horse. YOU'RE LATE! Oh, he says, the traffic was crazy. . . .

When I was in college my roommates and I loved to talk about the lives we would have someday: our award-winning careers, the guys we would marry, the children we planned on, a girl and a boy, as if delivery were guaranteed.

CYNTHIA GRANT

They say God always answers prayers. Why did He say no to me?

Compared to most of the people in the world, my life is a piece of cake. A great big slab. With ice cream, please. Whining when I come home from the grocery store because there's too much food to fit in the cupboards. If only there were more cupboards! Then I'd be happy!

We're talking tragedy, folks. Major inconvenience.

I've got so much to be thankful for: family and friends, good health, enough money, a car that usually runs, a home.

And a job that is driving me insane.

Forget about the job. Focus only on this moment, on the air flowing into and out of your nose, like a river flowing to the sea. Inhabit the eternal, the living present. Embrace infinity.

And tomorrow don't forget to ask Janessa if it's true she's engaged to that pimp she's been seeing.

CHAPTER EIGHTEEN

Her mother was going to blow, she could feel it.

She hadn't taken off her coat since she'd come home from work. She sat at the kitchen table, smoking, while Don explained why it was such a rip-off that he'd been turned down for disability.

"You'd think with this back, and the whiplash too—"

A minor fender bender. He was planning to sue. He went on and on about the money they'd get, while her mother's eyes grew colder and harder.

Raina was sitting on the couch, watching TV with Brandy and Lyn, while Jimmy ate a big bag of chips.

"He won't want supper if he eats all that."

"He's all right," Lyn said.

"He's getting fat."

"Two-year-olds are supposed to be chubby. You don't know nothing about kids. Mind your business."

She didn't want to share a place with Lyn. She'd asked Granny if she could move in with her, but Granny said no. "I'd love to, honey, but this place is for senior citizens."

Lyn would have to do her share of the work. She wasn't gonna be no baby-sitter so Lyn could take off with her idiot boyfriend who hung around all the time when he wasn't selling crank. Lyn kept hoping she could live with him. So far he hadn't asked.

The baby tumbled around inside her. Calm down, baby. Did it know her voice? They'd said so, in that class she'd took. She'd missed the one about breathing and labor. Lyn said forget the breathing stuff; once the baby started coming you got through it any way you could.

"I thought I was gonna die," she'd said proudly. "You can't believe how much it hurts."

She'd told Raina about this girl she knew, or maybe she'd seen her on TV, who was pregnant and went into the bathroom to pee and the baby's hand was sticking out.

She tried not to spend much time at the apartment. She dropped by the Laundromat to visit Bert and sometimes she went to the library. It was too noisy to read at home.

Things would be different once she got her own place. But how was that going to work? She didn't have any furniture, not a thing for the baby. Her mother said she'd help. She'd help Lyn, anyway. She might like Raina better when the baby was born. A sweet little baby. Unless she'd messed it up. At least she wasn't worried about AIDS anymore. Her fingers shook so bad when she'd made the call, she could hardly punch in the numbers. Then cried with relief. Her mother had caught her, said: It's always a big drama with you.

She was trying to be good. Had only messed up once when she went to Kimmy's and Pam showed up with her kids. Queen of the junkies. Arms and legs like sticks. Even Kimmy thought the kids should be taken away. Pam got on the phone and called her mother for money, pinching the baby to make him cry. Hearing him, she said, made her mom feel guilty. The other little boy wouldn't say nothing to no one. He stood around with his jacket on backwards, the hood hiding his face.

Raina felt so bad, she'd had a cigarette. Then a beer. What difference would one make? Then some people came over with a bunch of wine, and the next thing she knew she didn't know nothing and the baby was floating in dreams.

Sometimes she wished she could unzip her skin and step out of it and run away.

Why had she come home? She'd been so stupid. Her mother didn't love her. That would never change. She pictured herself trying to explain it to the teacher: See, my family doesn't believe in giving a baby away to strangers. We'd rather keep it and mess it up ourselves.

"That's bullshit," her mother was saying.

"I'm just telling you how it went," Don said. "I told them I couldn't work, with this back. And now this thing with my neck. They don't listen."

Her mother went to the fridge and popped open a beer.

"Where's dinner?" she said.

"Wasn't nothing to cook."

"You're supposed to get food stamps."

"I'm gonna, pretty soon. But the caseworker said—"

"Don't you know you can't take no for an answer? Those people don't give a damn about you."

"There's leftover macaroni and cheese."

"And that's supposed to feed five people? Here I am, working my butt off all day while everybody else just sits around."

"They wouldn't give me nothing," Don said. "Not a dime."

"So where'd you get those cigarettes?"

"Buddy of mine. He loaned me some money."

"You don't got any friends."

"You calling me a liar?"

"You better change Jimmy," Raina told Lyn.

"Soon as this show's over."

"Come on, he stinks."

"Change him yourself, if it's such a big deal."

Raina scooped up Jimmy and took him into the bedroom. She laid him on the bed and wiped him clean. He wriggled with delight when she sang to him and looked into his eyes. Lyn's mind was always wandering to the TV set. The other day he wouldn't stop fussing and Lyn had spanked him and pushed him away. Raina figured out the label on his shirt was scratching and he didn't have a way to say it. She tore it off and he was fine, smiling at her, his baby teeth shining.

Little boy, she thought, you don't stand a chance.

Her mother was waiting when she came out of the bedroom.

"So what're we supposed to do about dinner?"

"I don't know," she said. "I can go to the store."

"You shoulda thought of that before."

"I didn't have any money."

"So I suppose I'll have to pay for it."

"Yeah. Unless your boyfriend's got a secret stash."

"Leave him out of it."

"Gladly," Raina snapped. "I'm sick of him coming in the bathroom when I'm in there."

"Try locking the door."

"Try kicking him out."

"I don't know what she's talking about," Don said.

"Ask Lyn. She knows."

"It's no big deal," Lyn said.

"Yes it is. You're just too dumb to know it. You want your kid around a guy like that?"

"She's lost it," Don said.

"You better shut your mouth," her mother said. To her. "If I kick you out, you got nowhere to go."

She saw the whole thing then, as if it were a movie she'd seen so many times, she knew what would happen next. Like standing in the road, in a dream, in a movie, watching a speeding car coming at you. But you can't move your feet; can't get out of the way. And you have these lines you have to say.

"The only reason you want me around is for Lyn. So she can use my money to get a good place. Or you'll get stuck with her and Jimmy."

Her mother's face got so mad and scary, Don looked like he wanted to hide under the couch, and Lyn and Brandy sat frozen, while the TV blared. But Raina saw the joy in her mother's eyes; the sweet relief of rage.

She had always been her mother's favorite; the child she most loved to hate.

"I shoulda never asked you to come back," her mother said. "I shoulda known you'd act like this."

"You're the one who's acting. You don't feel nothing. Not even for your own kids."

"You're crazy."

"It's like you're in some dream and you can't wake up."

"You are one ungrateful bitch."

"I'll tell you something else: A mother shouldn't talk to her children like that."

"Not unless they're assholes."

Her mother's eyes glittered, always the sign that the fuse had been lit. The other kids would hide while the one she hit cried. Unless it was her. The tears came later; in bed, wanting to die, thinking: God, please take me. Then she'd wake up the next day and it would start again.

But she wasn't a little child anymore.

"You don't know how to love us," Raina said. "I guess you would if you could. If you were in the mood."

"You stupid little shit. You moron. You slut. You think you're better than me because you go to school? You're nothing. Knocked up with some junkie's kid. Probably fucked it all up when you were using."

"Look who's talking."

"As of this moment you're out on the street. With all the other losers. That shouldn't be too hard."

"Not with a mother like you."

There was a flicker in her mother's eyes. A wound. Then they flared in an ecstasy of hate.

"I didn't want to have you. Tried not to. Didn't work."

"Good thing, or I wouldna been around for you to beat on, and watch the other kids when you passed out."

"Fucking liar."

"Seven years old. Why'd you leave me in charge? Were you so stupid or did you just not care? Yeah, I know you had a terrible childhood. Me too."

"You're sick. You've always hated me."

"Why couldn't you love me? Because I knew what you'd done? I loved you anyway."

"I'll fucking kill you if you don't shut up."

"Too late; I'm already dead. Why aren't there any pictures of me and Bobby?"

"Don't you dare bring that up. Don't even say his name."

"There's pictures of everybody else."

"Do you hear what I'm saying? I mean it, Raina."

"You act like he never existed. He did. Are you so ashamed?"

"I can't believe you'd do this." Her mother moved toward her. "After what you done. It's disgusting."

"I didn't do nothing wrong, Mom. I tried to wake you up."

Her mother was on her, hitting her face and neck. Raina hunched forward, protecting her belly. Brandy jumped up and grabbed her mother. Please, Mom, don't! Got knocked aside. Her mother slapped Raina, tore her hair and shoved her. She landed on the floor in front of the couch. She looked up; Lyn was staring at the TV set.

She climbed to her feet, pointing at her mother. "That's it!" she said. "That's the last time you ever touch me!"

"Get out of here! You think I want you around? You and that retard in your belly? You've probably screwed it all up, like everything else! You're nothing to me! You don't exist! You're dead!"

"Please don't make her go!" Brandy cried.

She took nothing with her; she just left.

CHAPTER NiNETEEN

Something awful happened tonight. Raina came by. I was brushing my teeth, then the doorbell's ringing.

She didn't have a coat. She sat down on the couch.

"How's it going?" she said. "Long time no see."

I could hardly bear to look at her, I felt so sorry for that baby in her belly.

"All right."

"Aren't you glad to see me?"

"I'm always glad to see you, Raina. I've been wondering how things were going."

"Fine. I been staying with my mom."

"That must be nice. She always sounded like such a fun person."

I shouldn't have said that. But seeing her made me feel so upset. She's not some story in the newspaper; another article about the tragedy of teenage pregnancies. She's real, and she was sitting on my couch.

And I wanted her to go away.

"Have you been doing any writing?"

"No, not lately. I been getting ready for the baby and stuff. Trying to think up names. It's important what you name a baby."

"Yes."

"What about Savanna? For a girl, I mean. Do you think that sounds too white trash?"

"No."

"That's what my sister was gonna name her kid, if Jimmy hadn't been a himmy. If it's a boy I might call him Douglas Stephen. That was his daddy's real name."

"I see."

"What were you gonna name your kid? If you'd had one."

It was like some hideous dream. "Oh, I don't know, Raina. That was a long time ago."

"I just thought, you know, you might have some ideas."

I said, "I kind of liked the old-fashioned names."

"Like what?"

"Kathryn, for a girl. Or maybe Grace or Hope."

"What about a boy?"

"I don't know. Maybe Warren."

"You'd name a kid that? Good thing you didn't have one."

"It's late, Raina. What do you want?"

I hadn't meant to hurt her. But I felt like she was torturing me.

"Nothing. I just thought I'd drop by and say hi."

She told me she and her sister were going to get a place, as soon as she got her AFDC.

"But she sits around on her butt all day, so I end up doing everything. It's a drag. So I was thinking it might be better if we didn't. You know, live together, I mean."

I'd known Raina long enough and well enough to know that we were done with the preliminaries.

"I been thinking about what you said, Miss Johnson."

"About what?"

"You know, the baby and stuff. How I'm too young to raise it by myself."

"You already knew that, Raina."

"Yeah, but things got kinda confused for a while. My mother thinks families should stay together. Till death do you part, if necessary. So I was thinking maybe we could stay with you."

"Me?" I couldn't breathe.

"It'd be my baby but you'd be here too, and if I'm doing something wrong, you could tell me."

"No, Raina. That wouldn't work."

"Why not?"

How could she even ask me?

"You think I could sit here and watch a sixteen-year-old girl—"

"Seventeen. I had my birthday last week."

"—watch a teenager trying to raise a baby? I can't."

"Do you think I'm such a moron?"

"No, you're a child. And kids can't be good mothers."

"I can."

"Not now," I said. "Maybe later. Maybe someday."

"After what, thirty years of therapy? I thought you might want us around."

"Not like that. If you want to talk about letting the baby be adopted—"

"Why, so you can steal it?"

"I don't want your baby, Raina."

"Don't worry," she sneered. "We don't got AIDS."

I had never felt so hopeless. "That's not it."

"You think I fucked it up. That's why you don't want it."

I wanted to physically throw her out; out of my house, my mind, my life.

"You think I'd take this baby and have to deal with your family for the rest of my life? They'd never leave me alone. They'd drive me crazy. For God's sake, Raina, give this baby a chance! You've got to put it up for adoption."

"I can't." She hung her head. "Don't you understand, Miss Johnson? This baby's all I got."

"I'm sorry, Raina. I'd like to help you, but I can't do what you want."

She looked up at me then, her eyes gleaming. "My mother threw me out. We got nowhere to go."

I felt sick to my stomach. "I don't appreciate this, Raina. I don't like being manipulated."

She shrugged and smiled. "Hey, I'm desperate."

"That's your choice, not mine. You can't stay here. That wouldn't be best for anyone. Not for you or the baby. Or me."

"Then I guess that's it." She stood up and stretched, her belly poking at her sweatshirt.

"Where's your coat?"

"Don't got one. It's not that cold."

I gave her a jacket, and she put it on. I was afraid to let her go into the night alone, but more afraid to let her stay.

"Let me give you some money."

"I don't want your money."

"I can give you a ride."

"Where?" she said. "I'll see ya."

That was hours ago. Every time I close my eyes I see that kid walking down the dark street.

Chapter Twenty

She went to Kimmy's that night, but two guys got in a fight and the manager called the cops and they made everybody go. She hung out in a video arcade full of crazies, trying to look bad so they'd leave her alone.

In the morning she called Granny. Granny didn't want to talk.

"I'm late for work, honey. I gotta go."

She heard Granny's lighter hiss, her lungs reaching for the smoke. She knew her mother had phoned as soon as she was out the door.

"She tell you what happened?"

"Oh, honey." Granny sighed. "Why can't you two just get along?"

"She hit me, Granny. She knocked me down."

"She says you started it. Why'd you do that, Raina? You know how she is."

"So do you." She had to wait until Granny stopped coughing. "She threw me out. I got noplace to go."

"What about your AFDC?"

"I didn't get it yet. I go back next week."

"Tell them it's an emergency. They'll put you up in a motel till the money comes through."

"Couldn't I stay with you? Just for a while?"

"Oh, honey, that's not such a good idea." Granny explained that having guests was against the rules. Too bad, or she'd be glad to have her.

"That's not true. You're just afraid she'll hit you too."

"Raina, why do you say stuff like that?"

"You know she does. I've seen her do it."

But Granny's tears were a curtain she could not get through.

She stepped out of the phone booth. Rain was falling, turning into beads on the teacher's coat. She went by the Laundromat. Bert gave her a few bucks and told her a long story, something about his first wife and Social Security. She couldn't follow it; her back ached, and the baby kept moving.

Was her doctor's appointment this morning? No, Tuesday. This was Monday. She checked the newspaper rack outside to be sure. The front page story was all about the mayor's new clothes. She read as much as she could above the fold and thought: This baby's got more than one family.

She took the bus downtown, watching people on the sidewalk, their faces pinched shut, bodies hunched against the cold. It was warm inside the bus. She should just keep riding. But she made herself get off at City Hall.

It was even bigger than the welfare building. There were security guards and lots of people with briefcases. She took the elevator up to seventh floor and found the City Attorney's office.

The receptionist said, "May I help you?"

"I want to see Douglas Peterson."

The woman looked surprised. "He's expecting you?"

"No."

"I'm sorry, he has to be in court this morning."

"That's okay. This won't take long."

"May I ask what this is concerning?"

"His son."

The woman frowned and went into another office. In a moment a man in a suit came out. His eyes were very blue, and his hair was gray. That's how Sonny would've looked someday, she thought. When he saw her his eyebrows narrowed into an arrow. He waved her through the door into his office.

"Sit down."

He sat behind his desk. She looked around. The room was bigger than her mother's apartment.

"What about my son? He's dead, you know."

"Yes." The words she'd planned to say stuck to her tongue. "I just thought you'd like to know—Sonny was my boyfriend."

The way he looked at her, then. At her stomach, her clothes. As if she'd told the most disgusting joke.

"And I suppose you're going to tell me that's his baby."

"Yeah."

He picked up a pen, tapped his desk, put it down. "Do you know what I do for a living?"

"Sorta. Sonny said—"

"I'm a lawyer. An attorney. Ring a bell? You think you can walk in here and give me some story—"

"It's true," she said. "You can do a test. Check the

baby's blood or something. You can tell."

"Then what? Maybe you could come and live in my home. Or maybe I'll give you some money for your drugs. Is that what you were thinking?"

"No." She didn't know what she'd expected, didn't know why she'd come. "It's your grandchild. Sonny's baby. Don't you care?"

"Do you have any idea—no, of course you don't. How old are you, anyway?"

"Twenty."

He swiveled his chair around and stared out the window at the city spread below. He said, "My son was dead to me a long time ago. Long before you ever met him."

There were pictures on his desk, of a beautiful woman, and of Sonny's sisters, in graduation gowns and dresses. There were no pictures of Sonny.

He turned to her again, his voice as flat as his expression.

"I don't ever want to hear from you again," he said. "No letters, no phone calls, no visits to the office. And don't try to call my wife or come by the house. She's suffered enough. Do I make myself clear?"

She didn't move. Couldn't. She just sat in the chair.

"What did you expect?" He sounded so helpless. His empty hands were spread.

"Nothing. I don't know."

"I'm sorry," he said. "I can't help you."

He was standing, waiting. At the door she said, "You didn't even ask me my name."

"Does it matter?"

A security guard stood outside in the hall.

"Don't worry," she told him, "I can find my own way."

* * *

The shelters were full, but the last one took her in when the man at the door saw her belly. He gave her a cot and a towel and a toothbrush. The room with the beds was big and empty; the people had to leave during the day.

"So they can look for jobs," the guy explained. "The bathroom's over there. Don't touch nobody's stuff."

She stretched out and tried to sleep, but her eyes wouldn't close. There was nothing to read so she stared at the ceiling, trying not to think, to disappear; like when she was a kid and her mother had whipped her and she'd lain on her bed, melting into the mattress, dissolving into darkness, her arms and legs gone, absorbed into the bed, becoming the blackness, her mind shattered, somewhere else. I'm not here.

At seven o'clock they let the people back in, the men in one room, women and kids in the other. The girl in the next bed had a baby in a stroller and a boy about four with curly brown hair. He reminded her of Bobby. The baby was asleep; the girl put her in a crib and tucked the boy into bed. He kept asking questions: "Who's dat, Mommy? Where's she going?" She said, "Close your eyes, honey," and rubbed his back until he slept.

Beside the girl's bed were two framed pictures, of herself and the kids, and of her parents, Raina guessed. The girl rummaged through the plastic sacks beneath her bed. Then she began to brush her long blond hair.

"Hi." She smiled at Raina. "You're new here."

"Yeah."

"When's your baby due?"

"Anytime. I'm Raina."

"Jennifer." The girl wrinkled her nose. "Call me Jenny. Too bad people can't choose their own names. Like when you get older, you could be who you want. What would you choose?"

"I don't know."

"I'd choose Ashley. That's my baby's name. My little boy's Troy."

"He's darling," Raina said.

"He's a doll baby." The girl's hair gleamed golden. Everyone else in the room looked gray. "How'd you end up here?"

"It's a long story."

"Tell me about it." Jenny rolled her eyes. She told Raina how she'd planned to move back to Indiana and had saved up the money but her friend had ripped her off. "My friend, can you believe it?" Then the landlord kicked her out and didn't even give her notice. Which was totally illegal. And it wasn't her fault; she'd let some friends stay with her, and they got rowdy and the neighbors told the landlord they were selling dope. Which was totally untrue. But he kicked her out anyway and kept her deposit. As soon as she could afford a lawyer, she'd sue. Then she'd met this guy, Joey, and moved in with him. He was real sweet at first and he loved her kids. But he started getting drunk and beating her up. So she got another place and fixed it up real cute; painted it and always paid her rent on time. But for no reason at all, she hadn't done nothing wrong, the landlord threw her out. . . .

Raina could tell when people were lying; she stopped looking in their eyes because she felt embarrassed, like she was watching them do something sad and private that they didn't even know about themselves.

She's a speedfreak, she realized, wondering how she could've missed it. But the girl was fooling herself too.

Jenny said what she wanted more than anything in the world was to make a nice home for her family. Nothing big, nothing fancy: a little house with a yard so the kids could have their own room and play outside. Then she'd get a job and get off welfare, and when the kids went to school she'd join the PTA and maybe lead a Campfire troop. She'd been a Campfire Girl when she was little. In fact, her mom was still a leader back home.

"Here's my mom and dad." She showed Raina the picture.

"They look real nice."

The girl smiled. "They are. Do you got any family?"

"No."

"What're you gonna do when the baby comes? You can't stay here more than two weeks."

"Who'd want to?"

"It's not that bad. I was in one place where they let in all these winos. They howled all night, kept the babies awake."

Raina told her she was going to get an apartment, as soon as her AFDC came through. "Can't you get one too?"

Jenny explained that there'd been some big mix-up; they claimed she'd gotten more money than she should've, so they'd cut off her aid until she paid it back. Or something like that. It was complicated. Now she had to make sure they didn't grab her kids, because, "Once they get your kids it's real hard to get them back." They were her kids; no one else was gonna raise them. They weren't going to no foster homes. Some of them weren't too good.

"Yeah, I know."

All around them, people were getting ready for bed, herding kids back and forth from the showers and the bathroom.

"Boy," Jenny said. "I could use a smoke. Too bad you can't smoke here. It's just as well. Whenever I do, Troy says, 'Mommy, don't.' It's cute how he says it, kind of wagging his finger."

"What time do the lights go off?"

"They don't." Jenny shrugged. "That's the way it is."

Raina knew what the girl was going to say next, before she even knew it herself.

"Maybe we could get a place together," Jenny said. "I get food stamps. That helps. You'll get food stamps too. You could watch the kids, and I could get a job. I used to be a waitress. Made real good tips; one night I made sixty bucks! We could help each other out, take good care of our kids. They could kinda be like cousins or something."

"Maybe," Raina said. It wasn't a bad idea. You couldn't live on welfare, just starve. Jenny didn't seem lazy or crazy or mean. She loved her kids. Their clothes and faces were clean. Maybe she would love Raina's baby too. They could have Christmases together, with Santa Claus and stockings, and presents for the kids piled under the tree. And Thanksgiving dinners, around a big crowded table, with plenty to be thankful for, and eat; their kids grown up and happily married, with children of their own playing at her feet. She and Jenny would smile across the table and say, "And to think it all started in a homeless shelter!"

Was it so much to ask? Was it such a big dream?

"All right," she finally said.

"Well, all right! That's great!" Jenny laughed and they shook hands. "One thing for sure, though: I don't want no druggies around. The last place we lived, I had to keep Troy inside. There were needles all over; in the halls, in the park. I don't want my babies around that stuff."

"Me neither."

"You'll see." Jenny smiled. "It'll work out good."

At ten o'clock, the lights dimmed. Jenny turned on her side. Raina thought she was asleep, but then she said, "We got to find a place near good schools."

"Right."

"Troy's supposed to start kindergarten next fall. But I'm not gonna send him unless he's ready. Some people put their kids in school too soon. That's not good."

"No. Then they have to struggle to keep up."

"Exactly."

Jenny's breathing got soft and slow.

It felt odd to lie among so many strangers. What if someone went nuts and tried to hurt her? But even nuts need rest. The baby stood on its head. She rubbed her belly and whispered, "Go to sleep, little acrobat baby."

Night settled upon the rows of beds. A man coughed on the other side of the wall behind her head. A few women cried, but the kids were pretty quiet. Soon she was alone in a room full of dreams.

CHAPTER TWENTY-ONE

When she got up one morning something warm ran down her legs and a wave of pain washed from her head to her feet.

Jenny said, "Your water's broke! The baby's coming."

The puddle was pink. Jenny said, "There's blood."

Was that supposed to happen? She couldn't speak. Pain had always been outside, trying to break through her skin, but this was twisting deep inside her belly, her brain.

Jenny disappeared down the row of beds, then crouched beside her, rubbing her neck.

"Don't worry, honey. An ambulance is coming."

People crowded around, but she didn't care. She was alone in a place where there was only pain like she had never known.

"Try to relax. Take long, deep breaths."

Jenny sounded far away. A baby cried somewhere. Raina curled into a ball around a jagged stone of tearing, pounding, drowning fear.

Her brother's girlfriend had said it was like cramps, kind of achy and slow, then the baby popped out. I'm made to have babies, she'd added proudly. Yeah, like a cow, Raina's mother had said.

Jenny smoothed back Raina's hair. "Don't be scared, honey. The baby's in a hurry, that's all that's happening." A kid's voice said, "What's wrong with the lady?" Jenny turned away and shouted, "Where's the ambulance?"

Two men came with a gurney. They strapped her on it and wheeled her down the aisle, Jenny's face beside her. "Don't worry," she was saying. "Everything'll be fine. We'll get a place together soon as you get out."

Wheels clattered on the sidewalk. She was rolled inside a van, a man in a white suit busy beside her. A siren blared, or maybe she was screaming. The man attached something to her belly, her arms.

Then long white halls, doors exploding open, dark tunnels with lights flashing overhead, an elevator ride, then a small bright room, masked faces peering at her, fingers peeling off her clothes.

She had never felt so cold. She could not stop trembling. She clamped her teeth together, but the words squeezed out. "I can't do this! I gotta get out of here!"

"You should've thought of that sooner," a man's voice said.

They lifted up her legs, plunged something deep inside her. She fought them. The man said, "You've got to lie still!"

"Can't we give her something, Bill?"

"It's too late."

Was she dying? A woman's voice in her ear: "Can you pant, sweetie? Pant."

She'd forgotten what that word meant. Something gripped her arms.

"Prolonged deceleration."

"Get her over on her side."

"You've got to turn over, sweetie."

"I can't! It hurts!" Pain clawed at every secret place. Hands lifted her. She screamed. She faced a TV set. A green line stitched across the dark screen, bleeping.

"Down to eighty . . . seventy."

Something covered her nose. Bobby held out his arms to her, he looked so sleepy. He was closing his eyes.

"Wake up, Bobby! No!"

"It's oxygen, Raina." The nurse's voice. "We're trying to help you, but you've got to help too."

"Get her arm, will you—damn it!"

She'd knocked off the doctor's glasses. She tried to say, I didn't mean to.

"Nurse, do you mind? Are we on the same team here?"

"Sorry, doctor." The woman's urgent whisper in her ear again. "I know it's hard, Raina, but try to focus on your breathing."

She'd forgotten how to breathe.

"Will you hold her still?"

"I'll take over here, Bill." Another man's voice.

"Where the hell have you been?"

"In the john, do you mind?"

The doctors were talking, voices rising and falling like waves of roaring white-tipped pain that smashed her on an airless shore, then dragged her back to crash again.

The new doctor bent down and looked in her face.

His mouth and nose were masked, but his eyes were kind. "I'm Dr. Green, Raina."

"Where's Dr. Ramirez?"

"In surgery this morning. I'm taking her calls."

"She's all yours." The angry doctor left the room.

Dr. Green snapped on some gloves. "Raina, you'll have to forgive Dr. Miller. He hasn't been the same since his leeches died. He doesn't think little girls should have babies. Which is rather beside the point at this time."

The nurse laughed and said, "You're awful."

The doctor ducked behind the tent draped over her legs.

"I'm going to examine you, Raina. Try to relax."

"I can't! It hurts!"

"I'm not surprised. I can see the baby's suitcase."

"What do you mean?"

"I'm just joking, trying to put you at ease. Is it working?"

"No." But she was glad that he was there.

"I studied to be a comedian, but my grades weren't too good, so I transferred to medical school. Relax your knees, please. You're breaking my wrist. How long have you been a professional wrestler?"

"All my life," she moaned.

"You're doing good. Try to breathe through your nose. You're hyperventilating."

"What's that?"

"Freaking out." Then his hand was inside her, turning the whole world around.

"I'm gonna be sick!"

"You're doing just fine."

"It hurts so bad. Can't you give me something?"

"The baby's coming too soon. We don't want to dope it up."

"How soon?"

"An hour. Maybe less."

"You call that soon?"

The way she said it made them laugh. Her legs had stopped shaking, and there were breaks in the pain when she could catch her breath, then the pain would roll in again and overwhelm her. The nurse patted her arm and said, "You're doing great."

"I can't, I can't—"

It was a song she was singing. The others were speaking a foreign language: presentation, dilation, scalpel, appease—

"I'm going to do an episiotomy, Raina."

"What's that?" she gasped.

"Widen the opening so the baby can come out."

"You mean cut me?"

"There's so much pressure there, you won't even feel it."

"I can't, I can't—" She was on the ceiling, looking down at the girl lying on the bed, thinking: What's she gonna do? She can't escape. Then the pain pulled her down, wrapped its red arms around her, sinking its teeth into her bones, her brain.

She was blind, she was dying. Her mind tried to hide, to find someplace safe where there was no more pain. But it got there first, opening every door for her. She could only go where the pain was taking her.

Then it stopped. Like that. Was she dead? A baby cried. She'd forgotten the baby. Was the baby all right?

She was too scared to look. "Is the baby okay?" What

if it was nothing but a knot of flesh, a tangled mess of alcohol and cigarettes and meth? And it was all her fault, she was the one who'd done it—

Dr. Green laid something warm on her chest.

"She's fine, Raina," he said. "Open your eyes."

So little. So red. Eyes scrunched closed, skin all wet. But alive and warm and blindly turning her head. The nurse helped the baby find Raina's small breast.

"She's okay? Are you sure?" She could not stop smiling, marveling at the miniature body, the delicate perfection of the fingers and toes. "Her face kinda looks like she's from outer space."

Dr. Green laughed. "They all look like that. She's a beautiful baby, Raina."

The nurse took the baby to a corner of the room and rubbed her with a towel and put drops in her eyes. The baby wailed, a tiny piping sound that stirred in Raina's heart and made her laugh and cry.

The doctor was busy behind the drape. He said, "You're delivering the placenta now."

She felt a cramp, then something big slid out.

"I'm going to stitch you up a bit. I promise it won't hurt."

She felt only joy, her eyes full of the baby. Her daughter, her little girl.

She shared a room with a big, friendly woman who'd just had her fourth boy. "I'll trade you," she said.

"No thanks." Raina smiled. "I like what I got."

"Me too." The woman's family visited and called. Flowers and balloons bloomed around her bed. Raina had a phone; she longed to call the teacher. She's so beautiful, she'd tell her. I wish you could see her. If you did, you wouldn't ask me to give her away.

She'd always thought that hospitals were quiet places. People bustled in and out of the room all day. Volunteers in pink brought her magazines and menus. She chose whatever she wanted to eat. The food arrived on trays.

The nurses showed her how to bathe and feed the baby, and how to blanket her tightly so she wouldn't be afraid. Her milk wasn't in yet, but something else was coming out that was full of good stuff that protected the baby. She couldn't understand why Lyn had bottle-fed Jimmy, even propping the bottle on a blanket on his chest, when it felt so wonderful to hold and nurse your baby.

There was so much to learn. She had never been so happy. She wished she could stay at the hospital forever and teach girls like herself how to be good mothers. It's the most important job in the world, she'd tell them.

She held the baby for hours, just watching her sleep, breathing in the smell of her wispy hair, unwrapping the blanket to feel her skin. So soft. Like marshmallows, she told her roommate, laughing, the tiny fists curled tightly around her fingers.

Sometimes the baby looked right at her, her blue eyes calm and unblinking. I wonder what she's thinking, Raina thought. I wonder what she sees. I'm your mother, darling baby, precious little girl. And I'll never let anyone hurt you.

Things were going to change. Life was going to be different. She and Jenny would get a good place and fix it up. There'd be no junkies around, no people getting drunk. The kids would eat good food and get plenty of rest. They'd brush their teeth. Go to the doctor and dentist. They'd take a bath every day. She'd wash their hair. Their clothes would fit. Clean clothes, no stains. No shoes that pinched.

She wouldn't let them watch TV all the time. She'd take them to the library and read them books. They'd go to the beach and the park and the zoo. Maybe they could get a puppy or a kitten. It's your responsibility to take good care of it, she'd tell them.

There would be birthday cakes. Soft towels in the bathroom. Flowers in the yard and drawings on the fridge. When the kids got sick, she wouldn't act mad; she'd hold them on her lap and give them Popsicles and juice.

And when her mother said she wanted to see the baby, she'd have to promise not to smoke or drink or swear. She'd never go off and leave her baby there. There were always too many nuts around; guys you wouldn't trust with a puppy.

The next day Dr. Green dropped by. His mask had hidden a wonderful smile. He brought her a big bouquet of flowers. Her roommate said, "Will you look at those roses!"

Dr. Ramirez came to examine her, drawing the curtains around the bed.

"How are you feeling, Raina?"

"Kinda sore. But I took a shower. That felt great."

"Did you sleep last night?"

She smiled. "Not exactly. It seems like she's always hungry."

"I'm glad to see you're nursing the baby. Your nipples may get sore, but that will pass."

"That's what the nurses said. They're teaching me stuff. I'm gonna take good care of her. I am."

"I hope so, Raina. I really do."

Dr. Ramirez said the baby had tested clean.

She flushed. "I told you I stopped doing that stuff."

"Everything checks out fine so far, but there might be some problems later."

"What kind of problems?" Her heart felt squeezed.

"Learning disabilities, hyperactivity. That type of thing. It's hard to say. Maybe not; she looks good. She's a beautiful baby. You've been lucky, Raina. Don't press your luck."

"I won't."

"Is there anything you'd like to ask me?"

The doctor sat beside her while they talked. Then she patted Raina's leg and said, "Come see me next week."

A social worker came to talk to Raina. She asked where she planned to live with the baby, who was cuddled in a snug lump on her chest.

"We'll be staying in a shelter. Just for now. Me and a friend are getting a place next week."

"How?" the woman asked, trying not to frown.

"I'm on AFDC. We're gonna get an apartment. Or maybe a house. In a nice neighborhood. My friend's gonna work, so we'll have enough money. And I'll watch the kids. It'll work out good."

"Have you thought about adoption?"

Her arms tightened around the sleeping baby. "No."

"It might be the best alternative, in your position."

"I'm not giving away my baby."

"Have you ever heard of open adoption?"

"No."

"With an open adoption you could still be part of the baby's life. The parents would send you pictures—"

Raina cut her off. "No," she said. "I mean the answer is no."

The woman gave her a list of agencies that could help her, and said she'd arrange for some baby clothes and diapers.

"Thanks." She wanted the woman to go.

"Think about it, Raina. If you should change your mind—"

"I won't."

"Here's my card."

She left it on the table beside Raina's bed.

Her roommate had been pretending to read a magazine. "When's lunch going to get here?" she said. "I'm starving."

"Me too. I'll take good care of her. I will, I promise."

The woman smiled, but her eyes were sad. "I know you will, honey," she said.

Later, while she was nursing the baby, a secretary came to record information. She asked about the baby's father.

"He's dead."

"What was his name? We need to know for the records. And the baby might qualify for Social Security."

Raina pictured Sonny's father, his eyes brimming with pain.

"It coulda been a bunch of different people," she said.

The woman checked a box. "What's the baby's name?"

Raina looked down at the sleeping face; so innocent, so helpless, so full of fragile hope.

"Hope," she told the woman. "Hope Kathryn."

She didn't want to leave the next morning but it was time to go. Her roommate's husband had come to take her home. He tied balloons to her wheelchair and helped her sit down, then handed her the baby and an armload of flowers. Raina held her baby and the diaper bag of stuff that the social worker had dropped off that morning.

They rode down to the lobby in the elevator together. A volunteer in pink pushed Raina's chair. The lady was so old, Raina told her she could walk but the lady said no, that was against the rules.

The front doors gasped open. They were out on the sidewalk, the sky as blue as her baby's eyes. Her roommate hugged her and wished her luck, then rode off in a car with her husband and son.

The old lady said, "Aren't your people coming?"

"I guess they're late. Thanks for the ride."

She stood up, holding her baby and the diaper bag, and walked down the street to the bus stop.

Jenny wasn't at the shelter. People said she'd gone. She took her kids and left, they said; nobody knew where.

CHAPTER TWENTY-TWO

It felt funny not having any nurses around. There was no one to help, nowhere to put the baby down. She had to do everything with one arm, while the other held the baby to her chest.

The first night at the shelter, she hardly slept. She walked the baby so she wouldn't cry. Her body was exhausted but her mind felt peaceful. There wasn't time to think about herself anymore; the baby needed her every second.

For a couple of days it rained so hard people got to stay inside the shelter all day. The children played while the women talked or sat on their cots, their faces haunted.

Raina's milk was in but the baby was fussy. One woman said, "It's probably colic."

"What's that?" she asked. No one knew exactly, but it was something babies got a lot. Raina called the clinic and made an appointment to see Dr. Ramirez the next afternoon.

The baby was up most of the night. Raina held and nursed her, whispering to her as they lay on the bed. She could not stop looking at her baby's face. She had never seen anything so beautiful.

The next morning was cold but the rain had stopped. The shelter guy gave her a token for the bus. A lot of the passengers were sneezing and coughing. She shielded the baby's face with her blanket.

The welfare office was jammed and noisy. Some kids were running around in shorts. When she finally got to the front of the line the guy told her she'd missed her appointment.

"You were supposed to come in the other day," he said.

"I couldn't help it. I was having the baby," she explained.

"I'm sorry, but we're overbooked today. You'll have to come back tomorrow."

"Listen to me." She spoke quietly. The baby was sleeping against her neck. "We're staying in a shelter. We gotta get out soon. I'm supposed to get money so I can rent a place."

"I understand that," he said, "but I can't just write a check. You have to complete the application."

"I already did."

The woman in line behind her shuffled and sighed. The guy said her paperwork had been misplaced. She took a seat while he tried to find it. The baby woke up. She was hungry and wet. Raina changed her in the bathroom, spreading her blanket beside the sink. Then she sat in a stall and nursed and rocked her until the baby fell asleep.

The seats in the waiting room were taken. She paced around until the guy called her back and said part of the application was missing. They'd mailed some forms to her mother's address.

"I told you I don't live there anymore," she said. "We're staying at a shelter."

He explained that, in order to receive assistance, minors had to live with family members.

"Since when?"

"Monday."

"You're kidding."

"Does it look like I'm kidding?" His face was young but it hung in tired folds.

"My mother threw me out. We got nowhere to go."

"Are there other family members you could stay with?"

"No."

"Then you'll have to talk to a caseworker. I can get you in tomorrow morning at nine."

She stood there, stunned. The next woman in line moved up beside her.

"I'm sorry," the man said. "That's the best I can do."

She wanted to scream at him, to cuss the whole place out, but that would've woken up the baby.

They couldn't get back in the shelter until seven so they went to the Laundromat but Bert was drunk and when he saw the baby he got all worked up about his rotten kids and how they'd let him down.

The wind was blowing but she walked to the Square and hung around with some people she knew. The guys didn't pay much attention to the baby. The girls said she was really cute. It started to rain so they went to someone's house and it turned out Kimmy lived there too. She gave Raina a big hug and held the baby, a cigarette dangling out of her mouth. The ash above the baby grew long and white. She was glad when Kimmy gave her back.

More people came by. A guy was talking to Raina. His name was Tom, he was one of Sonny's friends. She liked his voice, so serious and quiet, and the way his eyes got when he looked at the baby. He asked if she'd mind if he came by sometime. She said that would be okay.

People brought pizzas, beer and wine. She ate a ton; she was really hungry. Kimmy said she could put the baby down on her bed. It was quieter in there. Raina tucked the spread around her. The baby fussed a little but she didn't wake up.

Raina took off her coat and sat down on the couch. Tom sat beside her and gave her some wine. I can't, she explained; I'm nursing the baby. His smile made her blush. He said, A little won't hurt. You've really been through a lot.

The wine untied her. She started to relax. It felt so good to be with people she knew. Tom said he hoped he wasn't being out of line but he'd always thought she was beautiful.

A little more wine wouldn't hurt the baby. Some doctors even said it was good for your health. She'd seen that on TV one time; something about heart attacks and stress. Tom said that he had heard that too. He brought her more wine and shared his cigarettes. She liked the way the smoke made her feel less empty.

She felt so good. She loved the baby so much! It was so important to be a good mother. The most important job in the world. Tom agreed completely. He listened when she talked. He didn't look at any other girls.

People told her they were sorry about Sonny. Man,

what a bummer. He was such a fine dude. Someone offered her a line, a little toot. For old time's sake. That won't hurt nothing. It burned up inside her nose like a cartoon fuse. The room got bright. Tom was holding her hand. It had been so long since anyone had touched her. Just doctors and nurses. Maybe he could be her boyfriend. She didn't care about the sex; that wasn't important. She just wanted someone to hold her.

Kimmy told a funny story about one of her landlords who'd screwed her over but she got him back. Raina laughed and laughed. She took another hit. Then another and another. She felt so strong. The way she used to feel a long time ago. Before Sonny died. He was dead. She was crying. Tom kissed her face and wrapped his arms around her. She kissed him back and her mind flew away, falling through silent space into darkness, the only safe place she'd ever known.

Something shoved her arm. An alarm was wailing. It wouldn't stop so she opened her eyes. She was seeing double; Kimmy's faces looked mad. She was holding out a crying baby.

"Didn't you hear her? She's been screaming her head off."

She couldn't focus. The baby's face was a blur of red.

"I been trying to wake you up. You gotta feed her," Kimmy said.

Something heavy was leaning against her arm. It was Tom; he was sleeping. She pushed him off and staggered to her feet, almost stepping on people. The windows were dark.

"What time is it?"

Kimmy held out the baby. "You better change her. She's soaking wet."

"I gotta get to the clinic. She's supposed to see the doctor."

"It even got on the bed," Kimmy said.

"Where's the clock?"

"We don't got one. Will you take this kid?"

She pushed past Kimmy and into the kitchen where people were talking. Nobody had a watch. Someone said to dial popcorn. She found the phone. A robot voice told her it was ten o'clock. The clinic was closed. She'd missed the baby's appointment. And the shelter was locked; she'd lost her bed for the night.

"What's the problem? You can take her tomorrow." Kimmy handed her the baby, who was crying so hard her face was blotchy and her arms and legs were twitching.

"I can't feed her," Raina said.

"Why not?"

"I used." Shame made her feel like she was going to throw up.

"It's not gonna hurt her just this once. You can stay if you want but you gotta shut her up. She's getting on people's nerves."

Raina clutched the baby tightly so she wouldn't drop her and stumbled into Kimmy's bedroom. She made it to the bed and tried to pull herself together but she'd gone too far away; she could not get back. Everything looked smeary and underwater. There were two howling babies in her lap.

She lifted her shirt and began to cry. The baby's hungry mouth found her breast. She sobbed as if she would never stop, as she watched her baby drink the poisoned milk.

Chapter twenty-three

The teacher was in the back room, getting ready to go home. When she came out the letter was on her desk.

Dear Miss Johnson,

I wanted to let you know how things were going, but I didn't know if you'd want to hear from me. Which is why you're reading this, not seeing me in person.

The baby's fine. She's doing great. It's hard to believe that she came out of me.

I've been around little kids all my life but never realized, until I had the baby, how truly vulnerable they are. It's like they're sitting in the backseat of the car and they just have to go where the driver takes them. Even if the driver's drunk or crazy or driving down the wrong lane.

I see these kids. They're with their parents, but they look lost: dirty clothes, no coats. Left in cars outside bars, faces pressed to the windows. Waiting and waiting. I want to save them. But where would I take them?

We stayed in a shelter for a while. Usually the longest you can stay is a week so we stayed with friends but the baby cried and that got on people's nerves. The doctor says it's colic because her stomach's immature. She'll outgrow it soon. She's nursing good. She gained three ounces last week.

It's funny not being alone anymore. Mostly it's good, but it's scary too. Before, it didn't matter what I did. Now I have to think about what's best for her, and figure out stuff like how to get diapers. They give out disposables at the shelters, but they say: These cost too much; use cloth. Well, that's just fine, but how do I wash them? Some laundromats charge two bucks per load.

I was supposed to get a place then things got all screwed up, so we're staying in a shelter now, over on Davis. They won't let you stay there during the day; you're supposed to go out and get a job. But it's not like people are dying to hire me. Anyway, what would I do with the baby? I know this girl who baby-sits. She parks the kids in front of the tube and splits. I go over there one time; the place was a wreck. Babies lying on the rug, crying. The kid in charge was ten years old, so that's out.

My social worker told me about a program for teenage moms. The babies stay in a daycare center while the girls finish high school and get their diplomas. They teach you stuff like nutrition and budgets and how to use computers so you can get a job. But there's a real long waiting list to get in, and she says the program might get dropped, so I don't know.

The other day my sister Lyn tracked me down. She said my mother was willing to take the baby because she doesn't want her living on the street, with me. She plans to run the baby through foster care. That pays a lot more than AFDC.

Bullshit, I said; she only cares about the money and taking away the only thing I got. She doesn't care about anyone but herself. Not you, not me.

My sister got hot. She said, That's not true! My mother loves me! Standing there, looking so huge and pathetic, hiding behind a wall of fat. You've always been mean and nasty and ungrateful! My mother's hate spilling out of her mouth. Screaming at me, right there on the sidewalk, people walking by staring. She don't care. She said: We'll call CPS and take the baby away.

You do that, I said. I want to talk to them too. I've got some heartwarming stories to tell them.

Since I had the baby, lots of guys come around, smelling welfare money and a free apartment. They tell you you're a special lady and they love the baby and on and on. It reminds me of those old cartoons where the wolf acts like the chicken's friend but there's a plate of steaming drumsticks over his head. It's hard not to laugh in their faces sometimes.

My mother's always had men like that. Gets rid of one and gets another even worse. When I was a kid I couldn't figure out why. I think she needs someone to despise, to blame for the way her life's turned out.

She said I made her nervous, always hopping around, acting silly and singing. I was trying to make her smile. She didn't want my hugs. I tried to talk to her sometimes, waiting until she was in a good mood; had had a little booze but not too much. I told her my father touched me. "You're a goddamn liar. Just making trouble."

I never told her about the others.

Once, I heard her tell a friend that if she had to do it over again, she wouldn't have kids; she'd get a job and travel. Her real life wasn't real to her at all. She didn't wash our clothes or help us with our homework, or join the PTA. She never voted. What difference does it make? she'd say. In the midst of all those kids, she lived alone.

It wasn't always that bad. But after Bobby died there was no turning back. The worse things got, the more drugs she took. The more she took, the worse things got. She tried to quit but she'd get so mean, we were almost relieved when she used again. Then she'd feel so whipped and trapped and stupid, she'd take it out on us. Mostly me.

She hated me because I knew what she'd done and she hates herself because she feels so guilty. So she tries not to think. She won't wake up. Her life is nothing but a long bad dream.

I tried to wake her up.

It's Bobby, Mommy. He's acting funny. He got into your pills.

She drank too much; she's passed out on the couch. The big kids are gone. Willie's playing with his truck and Bobby's asleep and I can't wake him up and I can't get the neighbors or call anybody because my mother always says don't call the cops. No matter what. She'll beat our butts. If the cops come around she might get in trouble. Then who'll take care of us? Granny? Are you kidding?

Don't you dare tell no one what goes on in this house. Not the neighbors, not the cops, not your teachers, not your friends. Don't even tell yourself. Get loaded. Pretend.

Mommy, wake up.

She finally opens her eyes. But Bobby never wakes up again.

I go over and over it in my mind. This time I'm running down the hall to the neighbors, or dialing 911 like they taught us in school. An ambulance comes, and my mom's not mad; she's glad I saved her, and Bobby too. Then everything gets better and she's smiling all the time. Smiling at me, like I'm her precious jewel.

If I hadn't been so scared of her, he wouldn't have died. He'd still be alive. So it's my fault too.

My mother hated Granny but turned out just like her. I don't want my baby growing up to be me. I love my baby. Too much to keep her.

That's why I want you to take her.

I know this is probably blowing your mind, Miss Johnson, but I swear I'm not playing any games this time. You always wanted a baby. There's nothing wrong with her. I don't know how, but she turned out fine. Don't take my word for it; you can ask the doctor. She said the baby might have some problems later, like being hyper, but she thinks she's going to be okay.

If my mother gets the baby she'll screw her all up, and I don't want her going to strangers. Some people seem fine, but inside they're weird. You're not. She'd have a normal life. That's all I want. I won't make trouble. I'll never change my mind and try to take her away. She doesn't even have to know about me.

She'll be all yours. I swear, I promise. Take me to a lawyer. I'll sign the papers.

I know this is asking a lot, Miss Johnson, but I don't

know what else to do. She can't stay with me.

If you want to take her, or think you might, and would like to talk about it, we're waiting outside. If you like your life the way it is, I understand, that's okay too.

Whatever happens, you treated me good, and I'm sorry I let you down.

The teacher finished reading and sat at her desk. A pool of sunlight slowly faded on the floor. She could hear her watch ticking. She could feel her heart beating.

Then she crossed the room and opened the door.

CHAPTER TWENTY-FOUR

For years I hoped I'd find a baby, like this woman in a movie I saw one time. She's jogging along, then she hears a sound; a crying baby in the bushes. No one else is around. The baby's been abandoned, but she's perfectly fine and the woman gets to adopt her.

It was almost enough to make me take up jogging.

All around me, kids were having babies, one or two students every year. When they finally have to tell you they're pregnant, their eyes plead: Don't be mad at me.

What can you say? Congratulations? To some fifteen-year-old and her nitwit boyfriend? I kept thinking that one of those girls would say, I know I'm too young to be a mother, Miss Johnson. Please take my baby.

That was years ago, when I believed in happy endings. Now some babies are born addicted, their little limbs twisted with withdrawal pains. Or the mothers drank, and the babies' brains are stunted. Sometimes you can't tell at first; the babies seem normal.

My cousin adopted an infant someone found in a car

parked outside a drug house. The mother was inside the house, dead; she'd overdosed. The baby seemed fine, but as she grew older, they couldn't control her. She'd fly into rages. She'd hit and bite, put her fists through windows, smiling as she held out her bleeding wrists. The doctors diagnosed a neurological disorder. They tried to subdue her with medication. Eventually she was placed in a group home.

My cousin's guilt has almost killed her.

Raina looked thin and dirty and sick. She sneezed and wiped her nose on her sleeve. The simple misery of a cold without Kleenex. I couldn't see the baby; she was wrapped in a blanket tucked against Raina's shoulder.

"Come in, Raina. Sit down."

"Thanks."

"Would you like a tissue?"

"Yeah." She blew her nose.

"I don't know what to say, Raina."

"That's okay. Do you want to see her?"

"Of course."

She folded back the blanket. The baby was sleeping, a lovely little girl, dark lashes brushing her cheeks.

"Isn't she pretty?"

"She's beautiful, Raina."

"I'm sorry to kinda barge in like this, but things haven't been going too good lately."

"Yes, I gathered that from your letter."

She looked at me, waiting. What did she expect? That I'd say, No problem, I'll take your baby?

"What's her name?"

"Hope."

My body stiffened. "I've always liked that name."

"I know."

"You're not just saying that to make me take her?"

"No." She looked disgusted and hopeless. "I thought I was gonna get to keep her."

"What's her middle name?"

"Kathryn."

The baby squeaked, her fists unfurling then curling into shells.

"Well, that's a very pretty name."

"She's a real good baby. Ask my doctor if you don't believe me."

"I believe you, Raina."

"There's nothing wrong with her. They've done tests and stuff. But she can't stay with me. Something bad might happen."

"You didn't kill your brother, Raina."

She looked at me, shocked, then tears began to roll down her cheeks.

"You were just a little girl. It was your mother's fault."

"Yes, but Bobby—" She couldn't speak.

"I'm so sorry, Raina. You must've loved him very much."

She nodded; tears dropped on the baby's face. She brushed them off. I handed her a Kleenex.

"He must've been a lovely little boy."

"He was. He always"—she struggled for control— "He always loved me best," she said.

"I'm so sorry, Raina. I wish I could help you."

"I know it's kinda sudden." She dried her eyes. "But you wouldn't be sorry. She's a real good baby. I know I could trust you, Miss Johnson."

"Well, that's very nice, but—" Picturing the two of us at Back-to-School Night, or in checkout lines at the supermarket. What a beautiful child. Is this your granddaughter?

"I won't try to get her back. I'm not lying, Miss Johnson. I'll go away, I promise. She'll be your little girl."

"Raina, I appreciate your confidence in me, but I'm too old to raise a baby now."

This was true. But I was too ashamed to tell her the rest; that I was afraid her baby was damaged goods. Afraid this blameless baby was a ticking bomb who would blow up in my face one day.

"You're not that old."

"She deserves two parents. I can't give her that, Raina."

"Yeah, but that's okay. Sometimes things aren't exactly perfect, but they can still be pretty good."

She talked fast, desperate. The baby was fine. No problems at all. The doctor said. Unwrapping the blanket. Feel her skin, Miss Johnson. Isn't she soft? Trying not to beg.

If I'd given birth to a baby with problems I wouldn't have tried to give it back; said: No, this isn't what I had in mind. Do you have anything without handicaps?

I would've claimed that baby as my own and loved it with all my heart. But this wasn't my child.

"Don't decide right now. You can think about it. We'll come back tomorrow. Next week, if you want."

The baby stirred and opened her eyes. Her mouth was like a tiny pink bow. She yawned and turned toward her mother's breast. Raina lifted her shirt and fed her.

For years I'd watched the road ahead, waiting for the prince on the white horse to deliver my life, wrapped up like a present: A husband and children. Family pictures. Dance recitals. Little League games. Summer vacation. Trips to the beach. *Are we there yet? How much longer, Mom?*

My eyes ached from looking into the lonely distance.

The baby peeped. Raina patted her back, then moved her to the other breast. She kissed the baby, murmuring, "You're all right." The baby's tiny fist clasped her fingers. They were two little children, holding hands. Two little babies, alone in the world.

Those children broke my heart, and entered it.

"All right, Raina. I'll take your baby." I could hardly believe what I was saying. Fear wrestled wild joy. My teeth were chattering.

"You will?" Relief flooded her face. "That's great!"

"There's something else." My heart was pounding. "I want to adopt you too. If you'll let me."

She stared at me in disbelief. "You don't have to do that."

"I know."

"I'll be okay."

"You can't keep living on the street, Raina. You're a wonderful girl. Won't you let me help you?"

She shook her head. "It wouldn't work out. I'm used to being on my own."

"Me too." I was as scared as she was. I could picture my mother's face: *Peggy, what are you doing? You're ruining your life! Who knows how these children will turn out?*

Not me; they don't come with guarantees. You don't always get what you expect. Sometimes you do but you just don't recognize it, because you're looking down the road for something else.

"I've done bad stuff," Raina said. "You don't really know me."

"I know everything I need to know. I'm not asking you to make a decision now. It might be harder than you think to give up your family."

"No," she said. "They gave me up a long time ago." Her eyes were full of doubt and hope. "You said it wouldn't work, me living there with the baby."

"Not if you were trying to raise her, and you won't. We won't lie to her, Raina, but I'll be her mother. That's how it will always be. I'd like to be your mother too."

"I'm kinda old."

"Me too."

"You know what I mean. I'm not used to someone telling me what to do."

"It won't be easy." I knew she would test me. I knew she would have to struggle against me, hoping I'd never let her go. "We'll have to try really hard and promise each other that no matter what happens, we won't give up."

"I'm scared I'll let you down," she said. "I don't want you to end up hating me."

"That could never happen, Raina. I want you for my daughter. My very own."

She nodded. She couldn't look at me. She brushed her eyes with her sleeve.

The baby finished feeding. Raina patted her back until a burp popped out, then she said, "Would you like to hold her?"

I took the baby. My hands were shaking. The baby's bright eyes fastened on my face.

"You gotta hold up her head. Her neck's like spaghetti."

"Sorry," I said. "I'm kind of new at this."

"Don't worry." Raina smiled. "You won't break her."

CHAPTER TWENTY-FIVE

She got home before the teacher did and turned on all the lights so the house looked cozy. Then she sat at the table and did her homework, listening to the wall heater hum.

The front door opened and the teacher came in with the baby and a bag of groceries.

"Is there more in the car?"

"A couple of tons. Did you clean up the kitchen like you were supposed to last night?"

"It's spotless," she boasted. "You could eat off the floor."

"We'll have to if you didn't do the dishes."

The baby smiled when she saw her. Raina kissed her cheek, then went outside and filled her arms with groceries. So many bags, she had to make two trips. She spotted a box of her favorite cookies, the kind she used to steal.

Sometimes she was afraid they were living in a dream and the teacher would suddenly wake up, screaming: What are you doing in my house? Get out!

Then she'd touch the key the teacher had given her. She wore it on a string beneath her blouse.

"How was school today, Raina?"

"Okay, I guess. They made us do all this terrible stuff."

"Like what?"

"Sit at desks. Write papers. Study."

The teacher put the baby in her swing and wound it up. She rocked back and forth, watching them put away the groceries.

For supper they had chicken and potatoes and salad and some round green things. Brussels sprouts, the teacher said. Three meals a day. It still amazed her. Sometimes she'd wake up in the middle of the night and go out and just look in the refrigerator.

"How was work?" she asked the teacher as they ate.

"Really busy. I've applied for a leave of absence next year. Money will be tight, but that's okay. I don't want the baby in daycare all the time, and I'd like to be here when you get home from school."

"I'm a big girl now."

"Yes, I know. That's why."

The baby squawked and waved her arms.

"She smells the food," Raina said. "She always gets hungry when she sees us eat."

"She knows what's good. Don't you, baby girl." The teacher stroked the baby and wound up the swing. "How'd your appointment with the counselor go?"

"Great. I had her in tears again. She says my childhood makes her sad."

"Well, that's a help. Maybe we should find someone else."

"Anyway, what good does it do?"

"We've been all through that, Raina. It's settled."

They finished supper and cleaned up the kitchen, then the teacher bathed the baby in the sink. She looked astonished when she felt the water. She kicked and splashed and made them laugh.

While the teacher got the baby ready for bed, Raina wrote in her notebook at the kitchen table. The house was so quiet and peaceful and clean. Sometimes the quiet made her nervous. She was afraid she would do something stupid and spoil it, like yell: I can't do this! and end the suspense. The teacher's face mad and hurt and disappointed. Get out. Right now. I should've known you couldn't change.

Be back on the street, alone again.

But the weeks went by and she hadn't wrecked anything. The quiet had begun to seep inside her.

The teacher came in, cradling the baby. Her fuzzy yellow sleeper smelled sweet and clean. Raina nuzzled the baby's belly and she giggled.

"What are you working on? Homework?"

"No. A story, I guess. Or a poem. It's kinda weird."

"What's it's about?"

"A white horse."

The teacher smiled. "The kind that comes with a handsome prince?"

"It's not that kind of horse."

The teacher patted her shoulder. "I'll be interested to read it when you're done. If you'll let me."

"Maybe. We'll see how it turns out."

The teacher fixed a bottle for the baby, then tested it on her wrist.

"Just right," she said. "Say good night to Raina."

"Bye, baby." She kissed her, and they left the room.

Raina wrote for a while, then closed the notebook. She found them in the rocker in the baby's bedroom, rocking back and forth, the teacher softly singing. The baby's eyes were closed, the bottle still at her lips.

"Is she asleep?"

"Watch this." The teacher tried to move the bottle. The baby's eyelids fluttered and she started sucking. The teacher chuckled. "Isn't she something?"

"I'm going out for a while."

The teacher's head swiveled around.

"I mean," Raina added, "if that's okay."

"Where? Alone?"

"No, with my biker boyfriend. We're going to Tijuana to get married."

The teacher sighed.

"I'm meeting this girl at the library. We're working on something for school."

"Raina, you know I don't like you out at night. And you shouldn't make plans before checking with me."

"Okay. Sorry."

"You think that's funny?"

"No." But it was, in a nice kind of way. Before, no one cared where she went or what she did. She was on her own. Now she had a curfew. "I'll be home by nine-thirty."

"Nine," the teacher said. "How are you going to get there?"

"Walk."

"At this time of night?"

"It's only five blocks. Okay, I'll run. Will that make you feel better?"

The teacher smiled uncertainly. "I'm still trying to get the hang of this, Raina."

"I know. You worry too much, Miss Johnson."

"Raina?"

"What?"

"You can't keep calling me Miss Johnson."

"Why not?" She couldn't call her Mom. Maybe some-day. Maybe never.

"It just sounds kind of odd," the teacher said. "Let's start with Peggy and take it from there."

"Okay. That's fine. I'll see you later."

"Nine o'clock, Raina. Don't forget."

"I won't."

She bent down and kissed the sleeping baby, her lips brushing the teacher's hair.

CHAPTER TWENTY-SIX

THE WHITE HORSE
by
Raina Johnson

The white horse came into our lives one night
on the draft leaking under the front door.
Mama was holding it at the kitchen table
when Bobby and I woke up the next morning.

A tiny horse the color of burning ice
danced and pranced on the palm of her hand.
We'd always wanted a pet but we were poor.
"This one's so small, it won't eat much," she said.

Bobby longed to take it to school for show-and-tell.

"No," Mama said. "Someone might steal it.
The white horse will be our secret."

THE WHITE HORSE

Mama loved the white horse. Its tricks made her smile.
She didn't look tired after work anymore.
Outside, winter howled at the door while
springtime bloomed on Mama's cheeks.

The white horse loved Mama. It hated us.
It snapped at Bobby when he sat on her lap.
"You were teasing it, Bob. Get down," she said.
The white horse purred on her knees like a cat.

Soon the white horse was as big as a dog.
It followed Mama everywhere she went.
She didn't have time to help us with our homework.
The white horse gobbled up all her attention.

Some nights, they left the house together,
the white horse on a leash wrapped around her wrist.
"We don't like being alone," I told her.
"Take care of your brother," Mama said.

The white horse ballooned to carousel-size
with staring eyes and a frozen mane.
On crystal wings it flew around the room,
Mama astride its back, laughing.

The white horse grew bigger and bigger.

"He's eating everything!" Bobby said. All the food
in the fridge. In the cupboards too. The TV set.
Mama's paycheck. Bobby and I needed new winter
    coats.
"Stop whining all the time," she said.

Every night Mama flew on the bright white horse.
Some mornings she could not get out of bed.
She felt too tired to go to work.
Our voices hurt her head.

She forgot to pack our lunches and give us kisses.

Keeping a horse inside was against the law,
so our friends couldn't come to the house anymore.
Mama closed the curtains to hide the glow that
rose like steam from his shining skin.

Bobby and I had to turn away.
It hurt our eyes to look at him.

The white horse ate the couch and the dining room set.
It devoured Bobby's bike. It grew bigger and bigger,
filling the whole house, warping the walls,
crashing through the roof so the rain fell in.

Mama didn't notice. The sun was still shining
where she and the white horse were flying.

"We've got to do something," I told my brother.
I told my mother: "The white horse has to go."
"No," she said. "He's a wonderful pet.
He loves me and he's beautiful and gentle."

Enchanted, dreaming, Mama was blind.
She didn't see what we were seeing.
The white horse watched us with ravenous eyes.
Soon there would be nothing left but us for him to eat.

THE WHITE HORSE

One morning we found Mama on the kitchen floor.
Her eyes were empty and her hair was wild.
Bobby got scared and started crying.
"Mama, make the white horse go away!" he said.

It reared up beside him, fierce teeth flashing,
its hooves lashing out, striking Bobby's head.
Bloody tears trickled from my brother's eyes,
waking Mama, breaking the spell.

"What have I done? He could've died!" she cried.
We rushed him to the hospital. Doctors bandaged his
    head.
"What happened?" they asked, their faces angry.
"He fell," Mama lied, fear and shame in her eyes.

Bobby didn't say anything.

When we got home the white horse was hiding.
Mama knelt and held us close.
"I'm so sorry, children. Can you ever forgive me?
Tonight I'll make the white horse go."

He sidled out shyly, after dinner, his sleek coat gleaming
like living snow. Mama was sitting at the table,
paying bills. He nuzzled her with his velvet muzzle.
"Go away," she said. "You hurt my children."

"Come fly with me," he whispered. "You know you love me.
"I'll take you where you want to go."
"No," she said. "My children need me."
"You need me more." The white horse bit her.

She screamed in pain and struggled against him.
He bit again, his teeth like needles
that caged her wrist and pierced her skin,
tattooing her with beads of blood.

"All right!" she cried. "I'll meet you outside.
Just let me say good-bye to the children."
"Be quick." He galloped out, huge hooves pounding.
Mama slammed and locked the door behind him.

His eyes filled the windows. The thin panes shivered.
"LET ME IN! I PROMISE I'LL BE SMALL!" he roared.
"No!" Mama said. "You can't trick me anymore!"
She stuffed rags in the cracks where he'd first snuck in.

The white horse heaved his crushing weight against the
    walls.
His icy breath shrieked down the chimney.
He pleaded. He screamed. His hooves thundered on the
    door.
All night he raged like a storm, a fever.

When the sun came up, the white horse was gone.
Mama and the house were still standing.

Bobby and I were afraid to go to school,
afraid the white horse would sneak back when we left.
"I promise you, children, he's gone forever," Mama said.
She sent us off with lunch and hugs and kisses.

That day I couldn't pay attention in class,
scared that Mama and the white horse were flying,

so high this time, we'd never find her.
"What's the matter with you?" my teachers asked.

After school I found Bobby and we hurried home,
racing through the streets, Bobby holding my hand.
From way down the block we could see our house.
All the windows were glowing like candles.

"Oh, no!" Bobby cried. "The white horse has come back!"
I held him and said, "Please don't worry anymore. I will
never let him hurt you. I will keep you safe forever."

We were so afraid to open the door.

But the light inside the house came from Mama's eyes,
shining with a mother's love, pure as fire.
She gathered us into her arms like flowers.

We never saw the white horse again.

Mary Wolf

We hurl along the ribbon of Highway 1, tires screeching on the curves, almost flying. Beside me, my father is making sounds like an animal caught in the jaws of a trap. Far below us, the restless ocean glitters like the fan of silver water he jumped through to please me, a lifetime ago. We laughed so hard. Now he's someone I don't know. He's like one of those animals you see on the road, that's been run over so many times you can't even tell what it was.

When Mary's father loses his job, life changes for the whole family. As the weeks turn into months, Mr Wolf becomes ever more volatile and a catastrophe seems almost inevitable . . .